喚醒你的英文語感！

Get a Feel for English !

喚醒你的英文語感！

Get a Feel for English !

附 **1** 片相談甚歡 MP3

My offer stands at sever...
...verheard During th...

Negotiation

...ut it another wa...

總編審：：王復國

作者：：Jason Grenier

談判

900句典

搞砸生意太離譜

影響，並提升談判實力的第一人
劉必榮教授 必備推薦

談判必備清單
☑反應力
☑說服力
☑900句典

...win-win...

貝塔語言出版
Beta Multimedia Publishing

Preface

In my years as a member of the legal profession, I have come to appreciate the fine art of negotiation. Make no mistake about it, negotiation truly is an art—when done well, that is. The best negotiators make it look easy! Poor negotiation, on the other hand, is completely devoid of anything even remotely resembling artistry. Not only are poor negotiators painful to watch and a misery to work with; their ineffective negotiation techniques are often totally counterproductive. *Overheard During the Negotiation* will separate you from this group of rank amateurs. By internalizing this book, you'll ensure your place in the group of highly skilled pros that make reaching consensus a thing of beauty.

It goes without saying that one need not be a lawyer to be a skilled negotiator. With the notable exception of hermits, the rest of us negotiate all the time, be it with our families, neighbors, coworkers, landlords, customers, suppliers, or other people we encounter as we go about our daily business. An infinite number of situations require us to engage in verbal exchanges of "give and take" in order to accomplish tasks, get what we want, placate others, and preserve social harmony. Whether it's something as mundane as deciding what color to paint the kitchen, or something as complex as the terms of a multilateral trade agreement, negotiation is an inevitable reality of life in a collective society.

This book offers you the linguistic tools you need to be effective in all negotiation situations, but it is especially geared towards use in business settings. *Overheard During the Negotiation* also includes helpful strategic tips and techniques that I've found to be useful and productive. Section 5 specifically details these tactics.

Negotiating is not always about winning at all costs. The larger relationship between negotiating parties is often much more important than what is actually being negotiated at any given time. Moreover, there's a lot of truth to the old adage about attracting more flies with honey than with vinegar. That's why the focus of this book is on helping you reach a fair agreement with the person on the other side of the table. But business sometimes means playing hardball, and for those occasions that call for a stronger hand, you're also covered. From getting to the table and initial procedural issues, through agreeing, disagreeing, persuading, clarifying, and suggesting alternatives, the language you need to reach consensus is all here. I've also included sections covering topics such as meeting control and flow, prices, shipping, contracts, legal and policy issues and outcomes. If you make deals in English, you need look no further than this one comprehensive volume.

You already know what you want. Now, learn the language and tactics taught in this book and go get it!

Jason Grenier
Hualien, 2006

作者序

在我任職法律界的數年中，我漸漸地懂得欣賞談判的藝術。毫無疑問，談判是一門藝術——當談得好的時候。頂尖的談判專家可以讓它看來輕而易舉，相形之下，不理想的談判卻完全和藝術沾不上邊。技巧欠佳的談判者不但看來礙眼，共事起來更是讓人難受。他們缺乏效率的談判技巧經常會招致反效果。《談判 900 句典》可以讓你脫離這群門外漢之列。只要熟習本書的內容，你可以確保自己位於高明專家之列，讓達成共識成為一件美事。

無庸置疑的是，不是只有律師，才能成為一個高段的談判者。很明顯地，除了隱士，我們每個人無時無刻都在談判，不管對象是我們的家人、鄰居、同事、房東、顧客、供應商，還是其他日常生活中遇到的人。我們需要在各式各樣的狀況中，利用言語上「施與受」的交流以完成任務、取己所需、安撫他人並維繫人際關係的和諧。不論是平凡如決定廚房要漆什麼顏色，還是複雜如多方經貿協議的條件，談判都是群體社會生活中一個無可避免的現實狀況。

本書提供讓你在所有談判情境中得以有效協商的語言工具，但是其重心特別偏重在商場環境上。《談判 900 句典》另外還包含了我認為十分有用的策略訣竅與技巧。Section 5 便針對這些策略詳加說明。

談判的目的並非總是要不擇手段地求勝。在任何時候，談判各方的整體關係通常比真正在談判的事情來得重要許多，而且有一句老話說得

好，甜言蜜語遠比尖酸刻薄要來得吸引人。這就是為什麼本書的重點是在幫助你與坐在談判桌對面的人達成公平的協議。但是有時候做生意就是必須強悍，在那些需要比較強勢的情況，本書也提供了你所需的用語。從準備談判與一開始的程序議題，到同意、不同意、說服、澄清和提出替代方案，所有你達成協議所需的用語都包含在本書內。我也納入幾個章節討論諸如會議掌控與流程、價格、送貨、合約、法律與政策議題和最終結果等等的主題。如果你是用英語做生意，你只需要讀這本談判大全便已足夠。

　　你已經知道你要的是什麼，現在就學好本書所教的用語與策略，挺身去爭取吧！

傑森‧格里涅
二○○六年於花蓮

推薦序

隨著全球化腳步的加速，國際談判的重要性也不斷升高。不管你是要跟外國人打交道，還是被購併之後變成外商公司；不管你是要增加公司的利潤還是增加自己的個人價值，英文談判都是一個必備的能力。

但要增進這方面的能力，必須藉助好用的工具書，幫助我們快速掌握談判每一階段的實用句型。《談判 900 句典》正是這樣一本好書。實用，易查易懂，而且可以快速掌握。更重要的是它還配合介紹了一些談判戰術（請見「Section 5 策略」），剛好可以作為「英文」和「談判」之間的介面。

本書第一部分「pre-negotiation」（直譯：談判前），在學界我們多半將其稱之為「前置談判」的階段。因為在這個階段，也是在談判。雙方先遣人員就談判的時間、地點、人員、議程、及議題範圍進行談判。如果是「多邊」、「多議題」的談判，像國際海洋法會議，pre-negotiation階段經常會拖上一段不短的時間。在這段時間內，我們也會做一些小讓步，試試看對方會不會回報。同時測試我們內部對這個談判到底有多支持。如果確認對方會回報我們的善意，而我們集團內部（或國內）也願意給予一定的支持，我們才有可能往下走，進入正式談判的階段。正式談判開始後，前置談判階段就結束了。瞭解這點之後，你再看本書的Section I 就會比較有概念了。

貝塔出版社最近在談判英文的推廣上相當用心，讓我們在提升個人

全球競爭力上，有了最好的學習夥伴。謹推薦這本書給所有想要增進國際談判能力的朋友。

東吳大學政治系教授
和風談判學院主持人
台北市談判研究發展協會理事長
劉必榮

談判主題曲 (by Brian Greene)

There's what you want and what you get
There's what they have and what they give

And in between there's some tricks
And in between there's some risks

There's what they want and what they've got
There's what you have and what you give

And in between there's some risks
And in between there's some tricks

Negotiation 難不難？
因為要談判怎麼辦？
Negotiation 敢不敢？
I really don't know if I can
But now it's easy, 好簡單！

There's what you want and what you get
There's what they have and what they give

And in between there's some tricks
And in between there's some risks

Negotiation 難不難？
因為要談判怎麼辦？
Negotiation 敢不敢？
I really don't know if I can
But now it's easy, 好簡單！

翻譯 你們的想望和你們能得到的；
他們所擁有的和他們能給予的。

在這之間有些詭計！
在這之間有些風險！

他們的想望和他們已得到的；
你們所擁有的和你們所給予的。

在這之間有些風險！
在這之間有些詭計！

談判難不難？
因為要談判怎麼辦？
談判敢不敢？
我真的不知道我是否可以，
但現在它好簡單，好簡單！

你們的想望和你們能得到的；
他們所擁有的和他們能給予的。

在這之間有些詭計！
在這之間有些風險！

談判難不難？
因為要談判怎麼辦？
談判敢不敢？
我真的不知道我是否可以，
但現在它好簡單，好簡單！

單元說明與使用方法

第一次接觸
Making First Contact

2 討論共同目標
Discussing Common Objectives

- 依本書分類架構做成的側標。
- 用語的主題。
- MP3 軌數。
- 將你習慣使用的用語，在 □ 中打勾，下次你可更快找到它的位置。
- 灰字部分可以依照你所面臨的情境，以其他字彙替換，黑字部分可以當作句型背起來使用。
- 生難字解說。

查詢小撇步：先由 側標找到所需用語的分類，再由 去搜尋用語的主題，很快就可以找到你所需要的句子。

Contents

前置談判

Part 1 準備上談判桌

Part 2 安排時間與其他事項

程序性議題

談判基本用語

Part 1 談論現況

Part 2 建立立場與可能性

Part 3 要求釐清

Part 4 同意

Part 5 不同意

Part 6 建議替代方案

Part 7 說服對方

Part 8 說明你為何未被說服

Part 9 改變你的立場

Part 10 提議

Part 11 表達情緒

Part 12 改變氣氛

Part 13 會議控制與流程

特定的談判議題

Part 1 金錢

Part 2 時間

策略

Part 1 處於劣勢的談判

Part 2 處於優勢的談判

Section 6 結果

Section 1

前置談判
Pre-negotiation

NEGOTIATION

Part 1

準備上談判桌
Getting to the Table

第一次接觸
Making First Contact

表示有意談判時可以說的話。

☐ I see some real opportunities here. Let's talk.

我看這裏有一些大好的機會。我們來談談吧。

☐ There are some things we need to talk about.

有些事情我們需要談一談。

☐ You have something we need; we have something you need.

你們有我們需要的東西，我們也有你們需要的東西。

☐ I'm listening. You've got my attention. What do you propose?

我在聽。你引起了我的注意。你有何提議？

☐ You've piqued[1] our interest. Perhaps we should arrange to meet.

你挑起了我們的興趣。也許我們應該安排碰個面。

☐ We like what we see, and we're interested in talking about the possibility of ordering some of your fabrics.[2]

我們對於所見頗為中意，而且我們有興趣談談是否可能訂購一些你們的布料。

---

1 pique [pik] *v.* 引起（好奇心等）
2 fabric [ˋfæbrɪk] *n.* 布料

討論共同目標
Discussing Common Objectives

記得要把人和問題分開而論,以雙贏的結果為目標。下列說法可以幫你起個頭。

☐ We all want to avoid a long, drawn-out[1] legal battle.

我們都想避免一場漫長、拖泥帶水的官司。

☐ We both want an amicable[2] settlement to the dispute.[3]

我們雙方都想平和地解決紛爭。

☐ Neither of us wants to see the Dream Factory shut down.[4]

我們雙方都不想見到夢工廠關門大吉。

☐ It's in both our interests to reach an agreement on pricing.

在價格上達成共識對我們雙方都有利。

☐ We have a common objective here: maximizing[5] profits during an economic recession.[6]

我們在此有一個共同目標:在經濟衰退期間獲取最大利潤。

☐ A time-share[7] arrangement is something that would work well for both of us.

分時共享的安排對我們雙方都會行得通。

---

1 drawn-out [`drɔn`aut] *adj.* 延長的;拖長的
2 amicable [`æmɪkəbl] *adj.* 友好的;和平的
3 dispute [dɪ`spjut] *n.* 爭端;糾紛
4 shut down 倒閉;停工
5 maximize [`mæksə‚maɪz] *v.* 使增至最大程度
6 recession [rɪ`sɛʃən] *n.* 衰退;蕭條
7 time-share [`taɪm‚ʃɛr] *adj.* 分時段享有的

3 提議進行談判
Offering to Negotiate

下列這些說法可讓你離談判桌更近一步。

☐ We ought to schedule a meeting.

我們應該安排時間開個會。

☐ We need to sit down to hash out[1] the details.

我們需要坐下來徹底討論細節。

☐ We should really get together to talk about the possibility of a joint venture.[2]

我們真的應該碰個面談談共同投資的可能性。

☐ Let's go ahead and set up a meeting.

我們就著手進行並安排個會議吧。

☐ I think it would be best if we could meet face-to-face.

我想如果我們可以碰個面是最理想的。

☐ I'd like to arrange a time to meet with you to discuss the details.

我想安排一個時間和你碰個面討論細節。

---

1 hash out 徹底討論後解決
2 joint venture [`dʒɔɪnt`vɛntʃɚ] *n.* 共同投資；合資經營

4 接受進行談判的提議

Accepting an Offer to Negotiate

下列是回應「We'd like to meet with you.」的方式。

☐ Thanks for the offer. We accept.

謝謝你的提議。我們接受。

☐ Name the time and the place. I'll be there.

說個時間和地點,我一定會到。

☐ That's a fine idea. Count us in. We'll be there.

好主意。算我們一份。我們一定會到。

☐ I'll make myself available. / We'll make ourselves available.

我會把時間空出來。/我們會把時間空出來。

☐ Very good. I'm looking forward to it.

很好,我很期待。

☐ We've got a lot to talk about. I suspect negotiations could run as long as three hours.

我們有很多要談的。我覺得談判過程可能會長達三小時。

Part 2

安排時間與其他事項
Scheduling and Other Arrangements

5 選擇時間、日期與地點
Choosing a Time, Date, and Forum[1]

MP3 07

邀請別人上談判桌的經典說法。

☐ Where/When would you like to meet?

你想在哪裏/何時見面？

☐ How about tomorrow, at nine a.m.?

明天早上九點如何？

☐ Are you free at ten o'clock next Tuesday the tenth?

你下星期二十號十點有空嗎？

☐ I think it's best if we meet on neutral[2] ground.

我認為我們最好在中立的場所碰面。

☐ Would it be possible for us to meet at our Taipei office?

我們可以在我們的台北辦公室見面嗎？

☐ I suggest the Commodore[3] Hotel as a suitable location for our meeting/talks.

我提議 Commodore 酒店，那是我們會面/討論的合適地點。

---

1 forum [ˈfɔrəm] *n.* 集會場所
2 neutral [ˈnjutrəl] *adj.* 中立的
3 commodore [ˈkɑməˌdor] *n.* 艦隊司令；海軍准將

6 更改時間、日期或地點
Changing Time, Date or Forum

下列這些說法皆可在前面加上「Sorry,」或「I must apologize.」。

☐ I've got a scheduling conflict.

我的時間安排上有衝突。

☐ I forgot I had already made a previous commitment.[1]

我忘記我先前已經有約了。

☐ Something urgent has come up. I'm going to have to reschedule.[2]

突然有急事。我必須重新安排時間。

☐ Could we make it for Tuesday instead?

我們可否改約星期二？

☐ I'm not going to be able to make it to our scheduled meeting.

我無法如期參加我們預定的會議。

☐ I'll have to check my schedule and get back to you.

我必須看一下我的日程表，然後再和你聯絡。

---

1 commitment [kə`mɪtmənt] *n.* （商業上的）約定；許諾
2 reschedule [ri`skɛdʒul] *v.* 重新安排時間

7 擬定議程
Setting an Agenda[1]

☐ There're a few things we should make clear before we start.
在我們開始之前有一些事情應該先釐清。

☐ I've come up with a rough agenda. Tell me how this sounds to you.
我已經擬出一個大概的議程,告訴我你聽了覺得如何。

☐ We have a tentative[2] road map[3] for our discussions. I'd like to run it by you.[4]
我們有個暫訂的討論計畫。我想說給你聽聽,看你有什麼意見。

☐ I've done some brainstorming,[5] and I've come up with the issues that need to be addressed:[6] inspection, shipping, insurance, and storage.
我做了一下腦力激盪,想出這些需要討論的議題:檢測、運送、保險和倉儲。

☐ We need to address the following issues: one, the color scheme;[7] two, the menu; and three, the hours of operation.
我們需要討論下面這些議題:第一、色調的搭配;第二、菜單;第三、營業時間。

☐ Is there anything you can think of that I've missed?
你能不能想到任何我遺漏的東西?

---

1 agenda [əˈdʒɛndə] *n.* 議程
2 tentative [ˈtɛntətɪv] *adj.* 暫時的;試驗性的
3 road map [ˈrod ˌmæp] *n.* 計畫;準則
4 run sth. by sb. 告訴某人某事以知其意見

5 brainstorming [ˈbrenˌstɔrmɪŋ] *n.* 腦力激盪
6 address [əˈdrɛs] *v.* 討論;處理
7 color scheme [ˈkʌlɚ ˌskim] *n.* 色調的搭配

確認與會人士
Confirming Who Will Attend

☐ Who's going to attend from your side?

你們那邊誰會出席？

☐ Can I ask who you're planning to send?

可否請問你們預計要派誰來？

☐ How many people are on your team?

你們的團隊有多少人？

☐ Will George Harrison be able to make it?

喬治・哈里森能夠來嗎？

☐ Cristina Wang is going to represent us.

克莉絲汀娜・王將會代表我們。

☐ Unfortunately, I won't be able to attend personally, but Steve Brown will go in my place.[1]

很不巧，我無法親自出席，但是史提夫・布朗會代我出席。

---

1 in one's place 代替某人

程序性議題
Procedural Issues

NEG⬤TIATI⬤N

儀器、家具和設施
Equipment, Furniture, and Facilities

MP3 11

☐ Is there somewhere I can plug this in?[1]

有地方可以讓我插這插頭嗎？

☐ Do you have an extension cord[2] that I could use?

你有沒有延長線我可以用？

☐ You can plug your laptop in here.

你可以把你的筆記型電腦插頭插在這裡。

☐ If you need to make a presentation, you can use the projector.[3]

如果你需要做簡報，可以使用投影機。

☐ We don't seem to have enough chairs. Let me get a few more for us.

我們的椅子似乎不夠坐。我去幫大家再找幾張來。

☐ Washrooms are located out the door and to your left, down the hall.

洗手間在門外左手邊，沿著走廊走下去。

---

[1] plug in 把（電器用品的）插頭插入插座
[2] extension cord [ɪkˋstɛnʃənˌkɔrd] *n.* 延長線
[3] projector [prəˋdʒɛktə] *n.* 投影機

10 確保設施舒適
Ensuring Comfortable Facilities

☐ Are you going to have enough space there? Can I get you anything?
你們那邊空間夠嗎？需要我幫你們拿些什麼東西嗎？

☐ There's a smoking area on the first floor outside the main doors.
一樓大門外面有吸煙區。

☐ Would you be more comfortable if I closed the window/blinds?[1]
如果我把窗戶／百葉窗關上，你會不會比較舒服一些？

☐ Let me know if it's too hot or cold and I can adjust the air con[2] to make it more comfortable.
如果太熱或太冷請告訴我，我可以調整空調讓溫度舒適一些。

☐ Would you mind turning up/down the air con? I find it a little warm/cold.
你介意把空調調強／弱一點嗎？我覺得有點熱／冷。

☐ Is there any way I could move my chair out of the sun / further away from the vent?[3]
有沒有辦法可以讓我把我的椅子移到沒有太陽／離出風口比較遠的地方？

---

1 blinds [blaɪndz] *n.* 【複數型】百葉窗
2 air con [ˋɛr͵kɑn] *n.* 空調（air conditioning 的簡稱）
3 vent [vɛnt] *n.* 通風口

時間管理與休息時間

Time Management and Breaks

11

無論你想在談判開始或是討論當中宣布休息時間，下列說法都可派上用場。

☐ We'll break for lunch/dinner/refreshments[1] at three o'clock.

我們會在三點休息吃午餐／晚餐／點心。

☐ Everybody looks a little tired. Shall we take a break?

大家看起來都有點累。我們休息一下吧？

☐ Let's break for fifteen minutes.

我們休息個十五分鐘。

☐ Let's keep going until eleven-thirty.

我們繼續進行到十一點三十分吧。

☐ Can we hold off[2] on our break for another few minutes?

我們可以延後幾分鐘再休息嗎？

☐ What do you say we take a short break so we can confer[3] amongst ourselves?

你覺得我們稍作休息如何？這樣我們可以私下討論一下。

---

1 refreshments [rɪ`frɛʃmənts] *n.* 【複數型】點心
2 hold off 延後
3 confer [kən`fɚ] *v.* 商量；協議

12 出席
Attendance

☐ Is everybody here?
大家都到了嗎？

☐ Are we missing anyone?
有沒有人還沒來？

☐ Has anybody seen Andrew Flynn?
有人看到安德魯‧富林嗎？

☐ We can't start until Felix Turnbull gets here.
我們要等到菲利克斯‧騰博爾來了才能開始。

☐ We're just waiting for Mr. Luo to arrive before we get started.
我們只是在等羅先生抵達，然後我們就會開始。

☐ All right, it looks like everybody's here. Are we ready to start?
好，看來每個人都到了。我們準備好要開始了嗎？

Section 2 程序性議題

13 寒暄與介紹
Greetings and Introductions

MP3 15

☐ I'd like to welcome you (all) here.

我要歡迎你們（各位）來到這裡。

☐ I am pleased to have you (all) here.

我很高興你們（各位）能來到這裡。

☐ I'd like to introduce my team/associate(s).[1]

我想介紹一下我的團隊／同事。

☐ This is Grant Hart, our Sales Coordinator.[2]

這位是葛蘭特‧哈特，我們的業務協調員。

☐ I'd like to introduce Mary Chen, Head of the Marketing Department.

我要介紹一下行銷部主任瑪麗‧陳。

☐ Allow me to introduce the engineer that has been spearhead-ing[3] the project, Tom Anderson.

請容我介紹一直在主導這個專案的工程師湯姆‧安德森。

---

1 associate [əˋsoʃɪɪt] *n.* 同事；伙伴
2 coordinator [koˋɔrdn͵etə] *n.* 協調者
3 spearhead [ˋspɪr͵hɛd] *v.* 當……的先鋒；帶頭

14 準備開始
Setting the Scene

☐ As you all know, we're here today to talk about a distribution[1] deal.
如各位所知，我們今天來這裡的目的是要討論一筆經銷生意。

☐ I hope this meeting/these negotiations will bear fruit.[2]
我希望這場會議／這些談判會有結果。

☐ This meeting represents an opportunity for us to team up[3] and crush[4] the competition once and for all.[5]
這場會議代表著一個我們可以合力擊潰競爭對手一勞永逸的機會。

☐ I ask everyone to keep his or her emotions in check[6] and have an open mind.
我要請大家控制自己的情緒，保持一個開放的心胸。

☐ I hope we can put our differences aside and salvage[7] what we can from this situation.
我希望我們可以拋開歧見，看看如何挽救這個情況。

☐ I'm optimistic/confident that we can come to an understanding[8] on this matter.
我很樂觀／有信心，我們會就這件事達成協議。

Section 2 程序性議題

---

1 distribution [ˌdɪstrəˋbjuʃən] n. 經銷
2 bear fruit 有成果
3 team up 協力
4 crush [krʌʃ] v. 擊垮；壓碎
5 once and for all 一勞永逸地
6 keep sth. in check 控制某事；抑制某物
7 salvage [ˋsælvɪdʒ] v. 搶救；利用
8 come to an understanding 達成協議；取得諒解

15 討論目標與開始談判
Discussing Objectives and Getting Started

☐ There are a number of items on the agenda today.
今天的議程裡有幾個項目。

☐ Let's get started./Let's get down to business, shall we?
我們開始吧。/我們開始談正事吧,好嗎?

☐ The first order of business is deciding on a color scheme.
首要之務是決定色調的搭配。

☐ Our primary[1] aim is to agree on the terms[2] of the supply contract.
我們的主要目標是要在供應合約的條件上達成共識。

☐ We've all agreed that our main objective/priority[3] is to revise[4] the delivery schedule.
我們都有共識,我們的主要目標/首要工作是要修正送貨時間表。

☐ If we only accomplish one thing today, I'd like it to be an agreement in principle[5] on the composition[6] of the board of directors.
如果我們今天只完成一件事,我希望是在董事會的人選上大致達成共識。

---

1 primary [ˋpraɪmərɪ] *adj.* 主要的;首要的
2 terms [tɜmz] *n.* 【複數型】(契約、付款等) 條件
3 priority [praɪˋɔrətɪ] *n.* 優先;優先考慮的事
4 revise [rɪˋvaɪz] *v.* 修訂;修正
5 in principle 大體上
6 composition [ˌkɑmpəˋzɪʃən] *n.* 構成;組成

16 引用書面和投影資料
Referring to Printed and Projected Materials

☐ You'll see in front of you some materials I'll be referring to.
你們可以看到在你們面前有一些我會引用的資料。

☐ I'll draw your attention to page five of the handout.
我要請你們注意一下講義的第五頁。

☐ Take a look at the second page of the packet[1] near the bottom.
看一下這份資料的第二頁，靠近底下的地方。

☐ The production flow chart can be found on page seven.
生產流程表可以在第七頁找到。

☐ This graph[2]/table[3]/slide[4] shows import data from 2003 to 2005.
這個圖／表／投影片顯示二〇〇三到二〇〇五年的進口資料。

☐ If you'll look here, I've prepared a diagram[5]/chart[6]/visual[7] to show our yearly earnings by quarter.
如果各位看這裏，我準備了一個一覽圖／圖表／投影片按季顯示出我們的年收入。

Section 2 程序性議題

[1] packet [ˋpækɪt] *n.* 一份（資料等）
[2] graph [græf] *n.* 圖
[3] table [ˋtebl] *n.* 表
[4] slide [slaɪd] *n.* 投影片；幻燈片
[5] diagram [ˋdaɪə͵græm] *n.* 一覽圖
[6] chart [tʃɑrt] *n.* 圖表
[7] visual [ˋvɪʒʊəl] *n.* 視覺輔助材料（如：影片、投影片、幻燈片等）

保密
Confidentiality[1]

依照談判的主題，你可能會需要提醒對方不要將你們討論的內容告知他人。

☐ I'm telling you this in strictest confidence.[2]

我把此事當成最高機密告訴你。

☐ Nothing said here today should ever leave this room.

我們今天所說的任何事都不能走漏出去。

☐ This should not be discussed with/disclosed[3] to any third parties.

這件事不可以和第三者討論／洩漏給第三者知道。

☐ This information/material/file is for your eyes only.

這個資訊／資料／檔案只有你們看得到。

☐ These are trade secrets and should not be revealed[4] to anyone.

這些是貿易機密，絕不可以透露給任何人。

☐ As a preliminary[5] to our discussions, we'll need you to sign this confidentiality agreement.

在我們進行討論之前，我們需要你們簽署這份保密協議書。

---

1 confidentiality [ˌkɑnfɪˌdɛnʃɪˈælətɪ] *n.* 機密；保密

2 in confidence 秘密地；私下地

3 disclose [dɪsˈkloz] *v.* 洩露

4 reveal [rɪˈvil] *v.* 透露

5 preliminary [prɪˈlɪməˌnɛrɪ] *n.* 初步行動；準備工作

18 可公開和不可公開

On the Record and Off the Record[1]

☐ This is strictly off the record.
這是完全不可公開的。

☐ Don't tell anyone I said this, but your marketing department sucks.[2]
別告訴任何人我說過這個話，你們的行銷部真是太糟了。

☐ You can quote[3] me on this: We will not be undersold![4]
你可以引用我的話：我們是不會拋售的！

☐ I'll go on record[5] as saying I never discussed prices with Brad Braddock or anyone else at Yoyodyne at any point in time.
我要公開說明，我絕對沒有在任何一個時間點和布萊德·布萊多克或優優戴恩的任何其他人討論過價格。

☐ You said, and I'm quoting you here, "There will be no price increases in 2006."
你說過，而我在此要引用你的話：「二○○六年時價格一定不會調漲。」

☐ What you said about Mrs. Hu's work performance is a matter of record. It's in the minutes[6] of the last meeting.
你對於胡太太工作表現的評論是有記錄的。在上次會議的會議記錄中可以看到。

Section 2 程序性議題

---

1 off the record 不留在記錄的；不可公開的
2 suck [sʌk] v. 【口語】爛透了；糟透了
3 quote [kwot] v. 引用；引述
4 undersell [ˌʌndɚˈsɛl] v. 以低於競爭者的價格

出售；低於市價出售
5 on record 記錄上有記載的
6 minutes [ˈmɪnɪts] n. 【複數型】會議記錄

19 決定下一步行動
Determining the Next Course of Action

☐ What's our next step?
我們的下一步是什麼？

☐ Where do we go from here?
我們接下來要怎麼走？

☐ So where does this leave us?
那，這麼一來我們要怎麼做？

☐ The next logical step would seem to be calling George Jiang to ask for his input.[1]
合理的下一步似乎是打電話給喬治・江，請他提供意見。

☐ If we're going to put our plan into action, the first thing we need to do is find a suitable location for the new facility.[2]
如果我們要將我們的計畫付諸行動，我們需要做的第一件事就是替新的廠房找一個合適的地點。

☐ To my way of thinking, the (immediate) priorities are drafting[3] the contract and getting the promotional[4] campaign[5] underway.[6]
就我的想法，（眼前的）首要任務就是要草擬合約，然後推動促銷活動。

---

1 input [`ɪn.pʊt] *n.* 提供的建議、情報等
2 facility [fə`sɪlətɪ] *n.* 用於某目的或活動的場所或建築
3 draft [dræft] *v.* 草擬
4 promotional [prə`moʃənl] *adj.* 促銷的
5 campaign [kæm`pen] *n.* 宣傳活動
6 get sth. underway 進行某事

20 安排下次開會時間
Scheduling the Next Meeting

☐ This is (obviously) taking longer than we expected.

（很明顯地，）這比我們想像的還要費時。

☐ We should schedule another round[1] of talks.

我們應該安排另一回合的討論。

☐ We'll need to meet again to wrap things up.[2]

我們需要再會面一次好把事情作個結束。

☐ We'll have to continue this at a later date.

我們必須改天再繼續討論。

☐ Let's sit down again on Thursday/October 12.

我們星期四／十月十二日再坐下來談一次吧。

☐ At our next meeting on the twenty-third we can pick up where we left off.[3]

我們在下次二十三號的會議裡，可以繼續未完成的部分。

Section 2 程序性議題

---

1 round [raʊnd] *n.* 回合
2 wrap (sth.) up 完成、結束（某事）
3 leave off 停止（不再做）

談判基本用語
Basic Language for Any Negotiation

Part 1

談論現況
Talking About the Current Situation

21 描述市場或經濟狀況
Describing the Market or Economic Situation

依據你的底線來選擇下列的說法，為自己建立一個有利的談判立場。

☐ The market for flat screen TVs[1] in Taiwan is currently growing/shrinking[2]/stable/booming.[3]

台灣的平面電視市場目前正在成長／萎縮／處於穩定狀態／蓬勃發展中。

☐ Demand for electric fans is on the rise[4] due to global warming.[5]

由於全球暖化，電風扇的需求正在攀升中。

☐ We're in the midst of a(n) real estate[6] boom/economic downturn.[7]

我們正處於房地產熱潮／經濟衰退中。

☐ We've seen a steady rise/decline in demand for our systems.

我們已經見到對我們系統需求的穩定成長／衰退。

☐ Unemployment/Interest/Lending rates are up/down.

失業率／利率／貸款利率上升／降低。

☐ Canada's economy is growing/holding steady/stagnant.[8]

加拿大的經濟正在成長／持平穩定／處於蕭條狀態中。

---

1 flat screen TV [ˋflæt skrinˋtiˋvi] *n.* 平面電視
2 shrink [ʃrɪŋk] *v.* 收縮；減少
3 boom [bum] *v./n.* 突然繁榮起來
4 on the rise 上升中
5 global warming [ˋglobḷˋwɔrmɪŋ] *n.* 全球暖化現象

6 real estate [ˋriəl əˋstet] *n.* 房地產；不動產
7 downturn [ˋdaʊntɜn] *n.* 經濟衰退
8 stagnant [ˋstæɡnənt] *adj.* 不景氣的；蕭條的；停滯的

58 談判 *900* 句典

22 討論趨勢與市場前景
Discussing Trends and Market Outlook

☐ Wireless speakers[1] are the latest thing.
無線喇叭是最新的產品。

☐ Solar-powered PDAs[2] are a hot ticket[3] right now.
太陽能掌上型電腦現在是熱門商品。

☐ We anticipate a rise/drop in demand for sugar.
我們預期糖的需求會增加／減少。

☐ The market forecast for MP3 player accessories[4] is encouraging/upbeat[5]/discouraging/bleak.[6]
MP3 播放器配件的市場前景看好／熱絡／不看好／暗淡。

☐ With the change of season, we should see an upswing[7] in demand for portable[8] space heaters.
隨著季節轉換，我們應該會看見手提式空間加熱器的需求大增。

☐ Our market analysis suggests there's a niche[9] here that we can exploit.[10]
我們的市場分析顯示，此處有一項我們可以開發的利基。

---

1 wireless speaker [`waɪrlɪs`spikə] *n.* 無線喇叭
2 solar-powered PDA [`solə`pauəd`pi`di`e] *n.* 太陽能掌上型電腦
3 hot ticket 【俚語】熱門的人物、事物
4 accessory [æk`sɛsərɪ] *n.* 配件
5 upbeat [`ʌp,bit] *adj.* 樂觀的；興旺的

6 bleak [blik] *adj.* 暗淡的；無望的
7 upswing [`ʌp,swɪŋ] *n.* 上升；提高
8 portable [`portəbl] *adj.* 可攜帶的；手提的
9 niche [nɪtʃ] *n.* 利基（較小的一塊市場，由需要未被滿足的消費者組成）
10 exploit [ɪk`splɔɪt] *v.* 開發；利用

Part *1* 談論現況

23 討論問題與風險
Discussing Problems and Risks

☐ The biggest barrier[1] we face in hiring foreign workers is the visa.
我們雇用外籍員工所面臨的最大障礙就是簽證。

☐ There's a very real risk that the NT dollar might depreciate[2] against the greenback.[3]
有一個很大的風險，新台幣兌美元可能會貶值。

☐ By refusing Mrs. Stavro's offer, we run the risk of alienating[4] all her supporters in the process.
拒絕史塔羅女士的提議，我們面臨了一個風險，在這過程中她所有的支持者都會疏離我們。

☐ There are a lot of legal/regulatory[5]/administrative[6] hoops[7] to jump through in order to get the property re-zoned[8] for commercial use.
若要把這塊土地重新規劃為商業用途，會有許多法律／法令／行政上的程序要完成。

☐ The really difficult part is going to be convincing the Hsintien City Council of the merits[9] of our proposal.
真正困難的部分將在於說服新店市議會我們的提議有何優點。

☐ Of course, (let's assume) things might not go according to plan.
當然，（我們要假設）事情可能不會依計畫而行。

---

1 barrier [`bærɪə] *n.* 障礙
2 depreciate [dɪ`priʃɪ,et] *v.* 貶值；市價跌落
3 greenback [`grin,bæk] *n.* 美鈔
4 alienate [`eljən,et] *v.* 使……疏遠
5 regulatory [`rɛgjələ,torɪ] *adj.* 規定的；管制的

6 administrative [əd`mɪnə,stretɪv] *adj.* 行政上的
7 hoop [hup] *n.* 箍；環（jump through a lot of hoops 指通過一連串的特定程序）
8 re-zone [rɪ`zon] *v.* 重新分區
9 merit [`mɛrɪt] *n.* 優點

24 描述相對的協議處境

Describing the Relative Bargaining Positions of Parties

評估對手的處境，並擬出一套策略，就像是在下一盤西洋棋或是玩一局撲克牌。

☐ You've got us over a barrel.[1]

你們讓我們束手就範了。

☐ The scales[2] are tipped[3] (heavily) in the brewery's[4] favor.[5]

釀酒廠（大大）占了上風。

☐ It seems RedStar has you at a big disadvantage.[6]

紅星似乎讓你們屈居於非常不利的劣勢。

☐ I wouldn't want to be in your position.

我不會想處在你們的情況中。

☐ You're forgetting that we hold all the cards[7] here.

你忘了王牌全握在我們手中。

☐ Miss Wu is in the unenviable[8] position of owing the government nearly two million in back taxes.[9]

吳小姐處於一個非常麻煩的情況中，她積欠政府將近兩百萬的滯納稅款。

Part 1 談論現況

---

1 over a barrel 【口語】陷於不利的立場
2 scales [skelz] *n.* 【複數型】天平
3 tip [tɪp] *v.* 使……傾斜
4 brewery [`bruərɪ] *n.* 釀造廠
5 in one's favor 對某人有利
6 disadvantage [͵dɪsəd`væntɪdʒ] *n.* 不利；

不利條件
7 hold all the cards 握有所有的王牌
8 unenviable [ʌn`ɛnvɪəbl] *adj.* 不值得羨慕
的；麻煩的
9 back taxes 積欠的稅款

25 強調客觀標準
Insisting on Objective[1] Criteria[2]

為了雙方利益，可使用下列說法來建立一個客觀的立場，並據此公平地評估各事項。

☐ How would this look to an objective third party?

這在客觀的第三者看來會是如何？

☐ Let's put personal concerns[3] aside for the moment.

我們現在先把個人的考量放在一邊。

☐ Compare this price to the industry standard/average.[4]

把這個價格跟業界標準／平均比較一下。

☐ Take a step back for a moment and look at this situation objectively.

暫時先後退一步，客觀地看看這個情況。

☐ We need to assess[5]/evaluate[6] this against the other proposals that are on the table.[7]

我們需要對照正在討論中的其他提議來評估／評量這個。

☐ There's no comparison[8] between this project and the Lakeshore Park development.

這項計畫和湖畔公園開發案不能相提並論。

---

[1] objective [əbˋdʒɛktɪv] *adj.* 客觀的
[2] criteria [kraɪˋtɪrɪə] *n.* 【複數型】標準（為 criterion [kraɪˋtɪrɪən] 之複數）
[3] concern [kənˋsɝn] *n.* 關切的事；有利害關係的事
[4] average [ˋævərɪdʒ] *n.* 平均
[5] assess [əˋsɛs] *v.* 評估
[6] evaluate [ɪˋvæljuˏet] *v.* 評量
[7] on the table 討論中
[8] There is no comparison. 不能相提並論。

26 考量行動方案的優缺點

Considering Pros and Cons[1] of a Course of Action[2]

☐ **There are pros and cons to** signing a three-year lease.[3]
簽訂一份三年的租約有好處也有壞處。

☐ **The flipside[4] of the coin is that** the developer might balk.[5]
這件事的壞處就是開發商可能會卻步。

☐ **One factor to consider would be** what other companies in the industry are doing to respond to the rising price of oil.
一個要考慮的因素就是同業的其他公司如何因應油價的高漲。

☐ **We can't overlook the possibility that** the pension[6] fund will be exhausted[7] by 2020.
我們不能忽略一個可能性，那就是到了二○二○年退休基金就會耗盡。

☐ **There is a very real likelihood that** the government will revoke[8] Mr. Minowski's business license.
政府非常有可能會吊銷米諾斯基先生的營業執照。

☐ **One drawback[9]/advantage of such a plan might be** a drop in revenue[10]/a long-term partnership.
這種計畫可能會有一個缺點／優點，那就是收益下滑／獲得長期的合作關係。

Part *1* 談論現況

---

1 pros and cons　優缺點；正反雙方
2 course of action　行動方案
3 lease [lis] *n.* 租賃契約
4 flipside [`flɪp͵saɪd] *n.* 反面（通常指較不好的一面）
5 balk [bɔk] *v.* 猶豫；躊躇不前
6 pension [`pɛnʃən] *n.* 退休金
7 exhaust [ɪg`zɔst] *v.* 用盡；耗盡
8 revoke [rɪ`vok] *v.* 撤銷
9 drawback [`drɔ͵bæk] *n.* 缺點
10 revenue [`rɛvə͵nju] *n.* 收益

指出所提行動方案之不可行 MP3 29

Pointing Out the Futility[1] of a Proposed Course of Action

☐ It's pointless[2] to hire another expert to study the problem.
雇用另一位專家來研究這個問題是毫無意義的。

☐ It's a waste of time/effort/money/resources to redo[3] the layout.[4]
重做版面是在浪費時間／精力／金錢／資源。

☐ It's folly[5] to think we can compete head-to-head[6] against Uniregal.
認為我們可以和聯皇正面競爭是種愚蠢的想法。

☐ Surely you can see the futility of trying to market this product in Taiwan.
你一定可以看得出，想要在台灣行銷這項產品是白費力氣。

☐ Any effort to resist the wishes of the board of directors[7] will (likely) be in vain.[8]
為了抗拒董事會意向而做的任何努力都（可能）會徒勞無功。

☐ What's the point in opening a new branch when we're struggling[9] to turn a profit[10] at every other location?
當我們掙扎著要在其他每個地點轉虧為盈時，開設一家新分店有何意義？

---

1. futility [fjuˋtɪlətɪ] n. 無益；徒勞
2. pointless [ˋpɔɪntlɪs] adj. 無意義的
3. redo [riˋdu] v. 重做
4. layout [ˋleˌaʊt] n. 版面設計；規劃圖
5. folly [ˋfɑlɪ] n. 愚蠢（的行為）
6. head-to-head [ˋhɛdˋtuˋhɛd] adv. 迎面地
7. board of directors 董事會
8. in vain 徒勞無功
9. struggle [ˋstrʌgl] v. 掙扎；奮鬥
10. turn a profit 獲利

28 表達意見
Expressing Opinions

☐ As far as I'm concerned, the color of the background is immaterial.[1]
對我來說，背景的顏色並不重要。

☐ It's been our experience that customers prefer a brand name they're familiar with.
我們的經驗是，顧客會偏好他們熟悉的品牌。

☐ The way I see it, the first option[2] is preferable[3] to any of the alternatives.[4]
我的看法是，第一種選擇比其他的選擇都來得好。

☐ We're of the opinion that any suggestion of a pay cut[5] is tantamount[6] to a slap in the face.[7]
我們的想法是，任何減薪的建議都無異是打人一記耳光。

☐ It seems to me that Lumber King is determined to[8] do this the hard way.[9]
在我看來，木材王決意要挑難行的路走。

☐ We (don't) think now is the right time to go public[10] with the news.
我們（不）認為現在是公開這個消息的正確時機。

Part 1 談論現況

---

1 immaterial [ˌɪməˈtɪrɪəl] *adj.* 不重要的
2 option [ˈɑpʃən] *n.* 選擇（的自由）
3 preferable [ˈprɛfrəbl] *adj.* 比較好的；更適合的
4 alternative [ɔlˈtɜnətɪv] *n.* 可選擇的事物
5 pay cut 減薪

6 tantamount [ˈtæntəˌmaunt] *adj.* 相等的
7 a slap in the face 一個耳光；一巴掌
8 be determined to 決心要
9 the hard way 辛苦地；吃力地
10 go public 公開

Part2

建立立場與可能性
Establishing Positions and Possibilities

29 建立你的基本立場
Establishing Your Basic Position

☐ Our (main) priority is to set a production schedule.
我們的（主要）優先工作就是設立生產時程表。

☐ Our short/long term goal is to get our products on store shelves in Eastern Europe.
我們短期／長期的目標是要讓我們的產品在東歐上架。

☐ We're determined to reach a work agreement that's acceptable to both management and labor.[1]
我們決心要達成一個勞資雙方都能接受的工作協議。

☐ We need to amend[2] the contract to reflect the changes we've agreed on in the memo of understanding.[3]
我們需要修訂合約，以反映我們在協議備忘錄裡已經同意的改變。

☐ We're here because we recognize the need to settle[4] this claim[5] as quickly and painlessly[6] as possible.
我們之所以會在這裡，是因為我們體認到我們需要盡可能迅速且不費事地解決這項求償事宜。

☐ We're looking/aiming to establish a branch office in Singapore.
我們的目標是要在新加坡成立一家分公司。

---

1 management and labor 勞資雙方
2 amend [əˋmɛnd] v. 修正
3 memo of understanding 協議備忘錄（簡稱為 M.O.U.）
4 settle [ˋsɛtl] v. 解決（問題、紛爭等）
5 claim [klem] n. （依權利而提出的）要求
6 painlessly [ˋpenlɪslɪ] adv. 【口語】不費事地

30 確立你的立場
Validating[1] Your Position

一旦表明立場，你就必須鞏固它。你知道如何做到嗎？你可以下列這些說法為出發點。

☐ I'm sure you can see where we stand.

我相信你可以看出我們的立場為何。

☐ The underlying[2] rationale[3] for the quota[4] is to minimize[5] over-runs.[6]

這個限量數額背後的論據就是要將超量的部分降至最低。

☐ What I'm saying makes (perfect) sense if you think about it logically.

如果你依邏輯來思考，那麼我所說的是（非常）合理的。

☐ I'm sure you can appreciate the reasonableness of our request/position.

我確定你可以理解我們的要求／立場之合理性。

☐ The reason we must insist on F.O.B.[7] sales terms[8] is the language barrier that faces our staff when doing business in your country.

我們必須堅持船上交貨價格之銷售條件的原因在於，我們的員工在你們國家作生意時必須面臨語言的障礙。

☐ We'd like to increase the transparency[9] of the bidding[10] process.

我們希望增加競標過程的透明度。

---

1 validate [ˈvæləˌdet] v. 使有效；確認
2 underlying [ˌʌndəˈlaɪɪŋ] adj. 基本的；在下面的
3 rationale [ˌræʃəˈnæl] n. 理論的依據、基礎
4 quota [ˈkwotə] n. 分配的數量；定量
5 minimize [ˈmɪnəˌmaɪz] v. 使……減至最少
6 over-run [ˌovəˈrʌn] n. （時間、費用等的）超出

7 F.O.B. 船上交貨價格（free on board 的縮寫）
8 terms [ˈtɜmz] n. （協議、合約中的）條件；條款
9 transparency [trænsˈpɛrənsɪ] n. 透明（度）
10 bid [bɪd] v. 投標；出價

Part 2 建立立場與可能性

31

探知對手的立場
Learning About Your Opponent's[1] Position

☐ I'd like to hear more from you on the issue of copyright[2] protection.
我想聽你進一步談談著作權保護的這個議題。

☐ I'd like to know your thoughts on a joint[3] custody[4] arrangement.
我想知道你對於共同監護安排的想法。

☐ I'd like to get some input from you on the cover design.
我想聽聽你對於封面設計的意見。

☐ Could you tell me a little more about your business plan?
你能不能再多跟我說一下你的營運計畫？

☐ What can you tell me about the restructuring[5] that you're currently undergoing?[6]
關於你目前正在進行的改組，有什麼可以告訴我的嗎？

☐ Perhaps you could elaborate[7] on your short-term objectives in setting up this venture.[8]
或許你可以詳細說明一下你創立這家公司的短期目標。

---

1 opponent [ə`ponənt] *n.* 對手；敵手
2 copyright [`kɑpɪ,raɪt] *n.* 著作權；版權
3 joint [`dʒɔɪnt] *adj.* 共同的
4 custody [`kʌstədɪ] *n.* 監管；監護
5 restructure [ri`strʌtʃə] *v.* 重新組織；更改結構

6 undergo [ˌʌndə`go] *v.* 經歷；接受
7 elaborate [ɪ`læbə,ret] *v.* 詳盡說明（後接介系詞 on）
8 venture [`vɛntʃə] *n.* 風險投資；冒險企業

32 應付對方立場的改變

Dealing with a Change in Your Opponent's Position

如果對方突然說出「We're backing out.」或「This just isn't working.」，下面這些說法就可以派上用場。

☐ Let's not be hasty.[1]

大家不要魯莽行事。

☐ Why the sudden change of heart?

為何突然改變心意？

☐ It's in everyone's best interests to reach an agreement.

達成共識對每個人都是最有利的。

☐ Why the about-face?[2] I thought you were all gung-ho[3] about this.

為何突然來個大逆轉？我以為你們對這件事都很熱切。

☐ Hold on just a second. You can't back out[4] now because we have already hired a new team.

等一下。你們不能現在打退堂鼓，因為我們已經雇用了一個新團隊。

☐ I thought we'd (already) agreed that the first shipment would be made in October. What gives?[5]

我以為我們（已經）同意第一次的送貨時間會在十月。怎麼回事？

---

[1] hasty [ˋhestɪ] *adj.* 倉促的
[2] about-face 一百八十度轉彎
[3] gung-ho [ˋgʌŋˋho] *adj.* 【口語】非常熱心的
[4] back out 取消；放棄

[5] What gives? 【口語】怎麼回事？；發生了什麼事？

Part 2 建立立場與可能性

33 重述與重申你的立場
Restating and Reiterating[1] Your Position

☐ At the risk of repeating myself, there is no way we can agree to that.
雖然我可能是舊話重提，但是我們不可能會同意那一點的。

☐ To recap,[2] demand is expected to rise in the next two quarters, and we're in a prime[3] position to exploit a niche in the growing market.
我把先前說過的整理一下，在接下來的兩季裡需求預計會增加，而我們處於一個非常有利的位置，可以開發成長中市場的利基。

☐ Just to reiterate, I'm not saying that you should bear[4] all the delivery costs, but rather that they be apportioned[5] fairly between us.
我只是要重申，我不是說你們應該承擔所有的運送費用，而是說這些費用應該由我們公平地按比例分攤。

☐ I want to make sure I've made myself (completely) clear on this: there will be no wage rollback.[6]
我想要確定在這件事情上我有把意思說清楚（說得一清二楚）：不會有減回原薪的情形發生。

☐ To sum up, we're looking for a supplier in Hong Kong that can provide quality products, shipped to us in a timely fashion.[7]
總而言之，我們要在香港尋找一個可以提供高品質產品、準時送貨給我們的供應商。

---

1 reiterate [rɪˋɪtə͵ret] v. 反覆地說
2 recap [ˋri͵kæp] v. 重述要旨
3 prime [praɪm] adj. 最好的；主要的
4 bear [bɛr] v. 負擔

5 apportion [əˋporʃən] v. 分攤
6 rollback [ˋrol͵bæk] n. 減回原（低）價錢、薪資
7 in a timely fashion 按時地

重述與重申對方的立場
Restating and Reiterating Your Opponent's Position

MP3 36

☐ What you seem to be saying is (that) you're not really worried about the size of the ad, *per se.*[1]
你似乎是在說，你並不太擔心廣告大小這件事本身。

☐ Your position, as I understand it, is that the renovations[2] have to be completed two weeks before the grand opening.[3]
依據我的理解，你的立場是希望重新裝潢的工作一定要在盛大開幕的兩個星期前完成。

☐ You've made it clear that you're unwilling to accept an offer that doesn't include a housing[4] subsidy.[5]
你已經表明得很清楚，你不願意接受未包含住宅津貼的提議。

☐ You're obviously of the opinion that the only fair settlement[6] will involve a lump sum[7] payout.[8]
很明顯地你認為唯有全額給付才是公平的解決方式。

☐ You've made a case for[9] dropping Budd from the list of sponsors.[10]
你已經擺明了要將百威從贊助者名單中剔除。

☐ You seem to be in favor of/against working with that developer.
你似乎贊成／反對和那家開發商合作。

---

[1] per se [`pɝ`se] *adv.* 本身
[2] renovation [͵rɛnə`veʃən] *n.* 修繕
[3] grand opening 盛大開幕
[4] housing [`hauzɪŋ] *n.* 住宅（的供給）
[5] subsidy [`sʌbsədɪ] *n.* 津貼

[6] settlement [`sɛtlmənt] *n.* 解決；和解
[7] lump sum [`lʌmp`sʌm] *n.* 一次付清
[8] payout [`pe͵aut] *n.* 支出；花費
[9] make a case for 擺明擁護……的立場
[10] sponsor [`spɑnsə] *n.* 贊助者

35 當對方不願明白陳述其要求時

When the Other Side Hasn't Been Forthcoming[1] About Their Demands

☐ You've got to tell us what you want.

你們一定要告訴我們你們想要什麼。

☐ You still haven't told us what you're after.[2]

你們還沒告訴我們你們想得到的是什麼。

☐ I'm still unclear on what you're asking us to do.

我還是不清楚你要我們做些什麼。

☐ We've heard what you don't want. What do you want?

我們已經聽過你們不要什麼。那你們要的到底是什麼？

☐ How can we make this (little) problem go away?

我們要如何解決這個（小）問題？

☐ Before I can offer you anything, I need to know what you're looking for from our firm.

在我提供你們任何東西之前，我需要知道你們希望從我們公司得到什麼。

---

1 forthcoming [ˋforθˋkʌmɪŋ] *adj.* 願意把話說明白的
2 be after sth. 追求某事物

36 當對方不願明白告知資訊時 **MP3** 38

When the Other Side Hasn't Been Forthcoming with Information

☐ **This is all news to us.**

這些我們都是第一次聽到。

☐ **Why weren't we told/informed/notified?[1]**

我們為何沒有被告知／通知／通知？

☐ **Why didn't you tell us you'd already signed a deal with MacroHard?**

你們為何沒有告訴我們你們已經和鉅堅簽約了？

☐ **What could you stand to gain[2] by keeping us in the dark?[3]**

把我們蒙在鼓裡，你們有什麼好處？

☐ **Withholding[4] information like this from us isn't going to help matters.**

對我們隱瞞像這樣的資訊，對事情並不會有幫助。

☐ **Being secretive[5] is counterproductive,[6] under the circumstances.[7]**

在此情況下，搞神祕只會有害無利。

---

1 notify [ˋnotəˌfaɪ] v. 通知
2 stand to gain 可能獲得
3 keep sb. in the dark 把某人蒙在鼓裏
4 withhold [wɪθˋhold] v. 扣留；不給予
5 secretive [ˋsikrətɪv] adj. 喜歡隱瞞的；不坦白的

6 counterproductive [ˌkaʊntɚprəˋdʌktɪv] adj. 招致反效果的；產生不良後果的
7 circumstances [ˋsɝkəmˌstænsɪz] n. 【複數型】情況（常與介系詞 under 連用）

Part 2 建立立場與可能性

要求釐清
Asking for Clarification

37 當你不清楚涵義時
When You're Unclear About Meaning

☐ I'm not clear on what you mean by "exceptional[1] circumstances."
我不清楚你說的「例外情況」是什麼意思。

☐ I'm still a little unclear on the meaning of "exit route."[2]
我還是有一點不清楚「退路」是什麼意思。

☐ I'm sorry. What exactly does "fixtures"[3] mean in this context?
對不起。在此情境下,「固定物」到底是什麼意思?

☐ Could you explain what you meant by "effect modulation"?[4]
你可不可以解釋一下你說的「效果調整」是什麼意思?

☐ What did you mean when you said that managers would have limited discretion[5] to approve holiday leave?
你說經理們核准休假時的裁決權有限,這是什麼意思?

☐ I'd appreciate it if you could clarify/expand on[6] what you meant by "alter[7] the existing floor plan."
如果你能釐清/進一步解釋你說的「變更現有樓層圖」是什麼意思,我會很感激。

---

1 exceptional [ɪkˋsɛpʃən!] *adj.* 例外的
2 exit route [ˋɛgzɪt.rut] *n.* 退路(指投資人最終能夠實現獲利的管道)
3 fixture [ˋfɪkstʃə] *n.* 固定物;裝置物
4 modulation [.madʒəˋleʃən] *n.* 調整

5 discretion [dɪˋskrɛʃən] *n.* 自行裁決;判斷的自由
6 expand on 更詳盡地闡述
7 alter [ˋɔltə] *v.* 變更;更改;修改

38 請某人重述說過的話
Asking Someone to Repeat Himself or Herself

☐ I'm sorry, could you repeat that?

對不起，你可以再說一遍嗎？

☐ Sorry, I missed that.

對不起，那點我沒聽到。

☐ What was that?

你剛說什麼？

☐ Come again?[1]

你說什麼？

☐ Sorry, I didn't hear what you said.

對不起，我沒聽到你說什麼。

☐ Could you speak up[2] a little, please?

麻煩你說大聲一點好嗎？

Part 3 要求釐清

---

[1] Come again? 【口語】你說什麼？
[2] speak up 更大聲地說

39 要求經過驗證的資料
Asking for Empirical[1] Data

☐ I'd like to see some empirical data.

我想要看一些以實際經驗為依據的資料。

☐ Have you crunched[2] the numbers yet?

數字你整理過了沒？

☐ Do you have any figures to back that up?[3]

你有任何數據來證明那一點嗎？

☐ Where did you get these numbers/statistics[4]/figures?

你是從哪裡得到這些數字／統計數字／數據的？

☐ How did you come up with these calculations?[5]

這些你是如何計算出來的？

☐ Show me the money!

把錢變出來給我看！

■ 1 empirical [ɛm`pɪrɪkl] *adj.* 以實際經驗為依據的

■ 2 crunch [krʌntʃ] *v.* 快速處理資料或數目

■ 3 back up 證實；支持

■ 4 statistics [stə`tɪstɪks] *n.*【複數型】統計數字；【不可數】統計學

■ 5 calculation [ˌkælkjə`leʃən] *n.* 計算（的結果）

40 要求舉例與提供例子
Asking for and Providing Examples

要求舉例

☐ For instance? Example?

例如？有什麼例子？

☐ Could you give me an example?

你可以給我一個例子嗎？

☐ It would be helpful if you could provide an example.

如果你能提供一個例子，會很有幫助。

提供例子

☐ Take the following situation, for example.

拿下面這個狀況作例子。

☐ Let me give you an example to illustrate[1] (what I'm saying).

讓我給你舉一個例子來解釋（我所說的事情）。

☐ I'm trying to think of an example. Maybe you could help me out?[2]

我正試著要想出一個例子。也許你可以幫我。

---

[1] illustrate [ˋɪləstret] v. （以實例）說明
[2] help sb. out 幫助某人

41

確認你是否理解 1
Checking Your Understanding: One

☐ Let me see if I've got this straight.[1]
讓我看看我是不是弄懂了。

☐ Please correct me if I'm wrong.
如果我說錯了，請更正我。

☐ My understanding is that the shipment was delayed because of an equipment failure. Is that right?
我的理解是，送貨之所以會延遲是因為設備故障的關係。對嗎？

☐ So if I understand you correctly, you're saying that the consignment[2] should still arrive on time?
所以如果我的理解正確的話，你是說託運的商品仍然會準時送達？

☐ The way I understand it is that the supplier will be responsible for the shipping costs.
我的理解是，供應商將會負擔運送成本。

☐ You said you were open[3] to the possibility of a three-way[4] split[5] of the proceeds.[6] Is that correct?
你說你對於三方拆分收益的可能性保持開放的態度。正確嗎？

---

1 get sth. straight 弄清楚某事
2 consignment [kən`saɪnmənt] n. 託運；託售的貨品
3 open [`opən] adj. 開放的；不拒絕的
4 three-way [`θri͵we] adj. 三方的
5 split [splɪt] n. 平分
6 proceeds [`prosidz] n. 【複數型】收益

42

確認你是否理解 2
Checking Your Understanding: Two

☐ **Surely you're not suggesting¹ that** we should accept three thousand dollars and call it a day?²
你一定不是在暗示我們應該接受三千元，然後就這麼了事吧？

☐ **You can't (seriously) be saying that** we'd stoop³ so low as to condone⁴ sweatshop⁵ practices.⁶
你不可能是（認真）在說我們會自貶身分，對血汗工廠這種執業方式表示寬容吧。

☐ **Are you inferring⁷ that** we were somehow involved in the disappearance of the package?
你是在推斷我們與包裹失蹤有某種關聯嗎？

☐ **Based on what you told me, I thought** you were authorized to make the final decision on the reserve price.⁸
根據你所告訴我的，我以為你有被授權決定最後的底價。

☐ **Am I correct in assuming⁹** you've already met with Karl Veres?
我認為你已經見過卡爾．維瑞斯了，我對嗎？

☐ **I was under the impression that¹⁰** you'd already taken care of that.
我以為你已經處理好那件事了。

---

1 suggest [səɡˋdʒɛst] *v.* 建議；暗示
2 call it a day （今天）到此為止
3 stoop [stup] *v.* 屈尊；降格
4 condone [kənˋdon] *v.* 寬恕；原諒
5 sweatshop [ˋswɛtˌʃɑp] *n.* 剝削勞力的工廠

6 practice [ˋpræktɪs] *n.* 練習；實行；慣例；執業
7 infer [ɪnˋfɝ] *v.* 推斷；推論
8 reserve price [rɪˋzɝvˌpraɪs] *n.* 底價
9 assume [əˋsum] *v.* 假定；認定
10 under the impression that 以為

Part4

同意
Agreeing

43 承認對方的論點合理
Conceding[1] a Point

有時候你必須承認對手並非全然在胡言亂語。如果你聽到一個牢不可破的論點時,試試下面的說法。

☐ You've got a (good) point. / You've got a point there.

你說得(很)有道理。/你那麼說有道理。

☐ What you're saying is true.

你說的是真的。

☐ I'll grant[2] you that.

我承認你是對的。

☐ I can't argue with that.

我沒辦法跟你爭這點。

☐ There's no denying that.

這是無可否認的。

☐ You've hit the nail on the head.[3]

你說得一針見血。

---

1 concede [kən`sid] *v.* 承認(為合理的)
2 grant [grænt] *v.* 承認(某人說的話)
3 hit the nail on the head 一針見血

認可對方立場的正當性
Recognizing[1] the Validity[2] of a Position

MP3 46

當對方從一個合理的立場來談判，你便不得不使用下列的說法。

☐ Your position is a valid[3] one.

你的立場確實有根據。

☐ That's a valid point. / Those are all valid points.

這論點很合理。／這些論點都很合理。

☐ I can understand why you'd say/do/believe that.

我可以理解為何你會這樣說／做／相信。

☐ You're (fully) entitled[4] to hold out for[5] more money.

你（完全）有權堅持要求更多的錢。

☐ You're well within your rights[6] to refuse the current offer.

你有充分的權利拒絕目前的提議。

☐ It's true that it may be in your best interest to handle this in-house.[7] I'm not in the best position to judge.

的確，在公司內部處理這件事可能對你們最有利，但我沒有立場來做評斷。

---

1 recognize [ˋrɛkəg͵naɪz] *v.* 認可
2 validity [vəˋlɪdətɪ] *n.* 正當；有效
3 valid [ˋvælɪd] *adj.* 正當的；正確的
4 entitle [ɪnˋtaɪtl] *v.* 給與……權利
5 hold out for 堅持要

6 well within one's rights 有充分的權利
7 in-house [ˋɪn͵haʊs] *adv.* 在公司、機關、組織內地

45 全然同意
Agreeing Wholeheartedly[1]

☐ You're absolutely right.

你說得完全正確。

☐ I'm with you all the way.[2]

我完全同意你。

☐ You're right on the money.[3]

你真是一語中的。

☐ I couldn't agree (with you) more.

我再同意（你）不過了。

☐ We're in complete agreement (on this/that).

我們（在這／那一點上）意見完全一致。

☐ I'm in one-hundred-percent agreement (with what you've said).

我百分之百同意（你說的話）。

---

1 wholeheartedly [ˌholˈhɑrtɪdlɪ] *adv.* 全心全意地；由衷地
2 all the way 完完全全
3 right on the money 一語中的

46 同意但有所保留
Agreeing with Reservations[1]

MP3 48

☐ I agree to a point.[2] But I feel discontinuing[3] the line is a mistake.
我在某個程度上是同意的，但是我覺得中止這個產品線是個錯誤。

☐ OK, but I have some reservations about your choice of leadership.
好吧，但是我對於你選擇的領導人有所保留。

☐ I agree, in principle,[4] but I don't think it's going to fly with[5] my boss.
我原則上同意，但是我不覺得我老闆會接受。

☐ I'll grant you it looks like a good idea on paper, but I'm still not convinced[6] it's going to work.
我承認這在書面上看起來是個不錯的主意，但我還是不認為它會行得通。

☐ I agree with some of what you've said, but I still maintain[7] that our customers are going to notice the difference.
我同意你說的某些話，但是我還是堅決認為我們的客戶會注意到不同之處。

☐ We're in agreement with the general thrust[8] of your argument, but still have some doubts about the second stage of your plan.
我們同意你整體的主要論點，但是依舊對你計畫的第二階段有所疑慮。

Part 4 同意

---

1 reservation [ˌrɛzəˋveʃən] *n.* 保留
2 to a point　某種程度上
3 discontinue [ˌdɪskənˋtɪnju] *v.* 停止；中止
4 in principle　原則上；大體上
5 (not) fly with sb.　某人（不）會同意、接受

（通常為否定用法）
6 convince [kənˋvɪns] *v.* 使……確信
7 maintain [menˋten] *v.* 堅決主張
8 thrust [ˋθrʌst] *n.* 要旨；要點

Part5

不同意
Disagreeing

質疑某個論點
Challenging[1] a Point

當你聽到某個你無法信服或是不合理的論點，可以用下列的說法來加以反駁。

☐ I take issue with[2] that last point.

我對最後一點有異議。

☐ That's not true. / That's totally false.

那不是真的。／那完全不正確。

☐ I'm going to have to refute[3] what you just said.

我必須要反駁你剛才說的話。

☐ You said customers don't care. I don't buy[4] that.

你說顧客不在乎。我不相信。

☐ I can't accept that your costs have doubled in such a short time.

我不能接受你們的成本在這麼短的時間內增加了一倍。

☐ I'm not (at all) convinced that these measures[5] aren't going to affect the quality of the products.

我（完全）不相信這些做法不會影響產品的品質。

---

1 challenge [ˋtʃælɪndʒ] v. 對⋯⋯提出異議

2 take issue with 與⋯⋯爭論；與⋯⋯意見不合

3 refute [rɪˋfjut] v. 駁斥；反駁

4 buy [baɪ] v.【俚】相信；接受

5 measures [ˋmɛʒəz] n.【複數型】措施；方法

48 質疑立場的正當性
Challenging the Validity of a Position

當你發現對方的邏輯有問題，可使用下列說法來質疑他的立場。

☐ So what exactly are you arguing?

所以你到底在爭論什麼？

☐ I think you're (way) off base[1] here.

我認為你說的（完全）錯誤。

☐ I'm afraid I don't follow[2] your logic.

我恐怕不明白你的邏輯。

☐ I don't see how you can defend[3] your position.

我看不出你如何為你的立場辯護。

☐ You're losing[4] me here. That doesn't make any sense.

我聽不懂你說的。那完全不合理。

☐ I don't think it's fair/valid to say we haven't given you every opportunity to comply.[5]

我不覺得說我們沒有給你們充分的機會配合是公平的／合理的。

---

1 (way) off base 【口語】（完全）錯的
2 follow [ˋfɑlo] *v.* 聽得懂；跟得上
3 defend [dɪˋfɛnd] *v.* 辯護
4 lose [luz] *v.* 使弄不懂
5 comply [kəmˋplaɪ] *v.* 服從；依從

49 表達強烈不同意
Expressing Strong Disagreement

☐ That's absurd![1]

那太荒謬了！

☐ I totally disagree.

我完全不同意。

☐ That's absolutely false.

那完完全全不正確。

☐ I think you're wrong (about that).

我認為你（這件事）說錯了。

☐ You're being deliberately[2] deceptive[3]/misleading[4]/evasive.[5]

你一直蓄意欺瞞／誤導／避重就輕。

☐ That's simply not true/not the case. Let me show you why.

情況根本不是那樣。讓我告訴你為什麼。

---

1 absurd [əb`sɜd] *adj.* 荒唐的；不合理的
2 deliberately [dɪ`lɪbərɪtlɪ] *adv.* 故意地；有計畫地
3 deceptive [dɪ`sɛptɪv] *adj.* 欺騙人的
4 misleading [mɪs`lidɪŋ] *adj.* 使人誤解的
5 evasive [ɪ`vesɪv] *adj.* 迴避的；含糊其辭的

50 不同意但是讓步
Disagreeing While Making Concessions[1]

☐ I disagree, but I will concede that you should have been notified.
我不同意，但是我承認你應該要被通知。

☐ I doubt it, but I'm willing to put my doubts aside for the time being.[2]
我很懷疑，但是我願意暫時把我的疑慮擺在一旁。

☐ I'm (still) not convinced, however I'm willing to keep listening.
我（還是）不相信，但是我願意繼續聽下去。

☐ I don't agree with what you've said, but at least you accept partial[3] responsibility for the incident.[4]
我不同意你說的，但是至少你願意承擔這個事件的部分責任。

☐ I'm still not sold[5] on the idea of exclusive[6] distribution[7] rights, but I'm willing to consider it.
我還是不相信獨家經銷權是個好主意，但是我願意考慮。

☐ I (still) have reservations about the composition[8] of the delegation,[9] but I will grant you there are some impressive[10] names on the list.
我（還是）對代表團的人選有所保留，但是我承認名單上有一些很有分量的名字。

---

1 concession [kən`sɛʃən] *n.* 讓步
2 for the time being 暫時；目前
3 partial [`parʃəl] *adj.* 部分的
4 incident [`ɪnsədənt] *n.* 事件
5 sell [sɛl] *v.* 使人相信……是最好的
6 exclusive [ɪk`sklusɪv] *adj.* 獨佔的；唯一的

7 distribution [ˌdɪstrə`bjuʃən] *n.* 配銷
8 composition [ˌkɑmpə`zɪʃən] *n.* 組成
9 delegation [ˌdɛlə`geʃən] *n.* 代表團
10 impressive [ɪm`prɛsɪv] *adj.* 令人印象深刻的；令人欽佩的

Part 5 不同意

Part 6

建議替代方案
Suggesting Alternatives

51 找出癥結
Identifying Sticking Points[1]

☐ The production schedule is a sticking point.

生產時程表是個癥結。

☐ We seem to be getting hung up[2] on the issue of lead times.[3]

我們似乎在交貨前置時間的問題上遇到了瓶頸。

☐ The only thing we haven't resolved is responsibility for insurance.

我們唯一還沒解決的事情就是保險的責任歸屬問題。

☐ The scope[4] of the license is the one outstanding[5] issue.

執照範圍就是唯一尚未解決的問題。

☐ We can't move forward until we settle on[6] the terms of sale.

我們要先在銷售條件上達成共識，否則就不能繼續談下去。

☐ We seem to be at an impasse[7] on the issue of the lease's duration.[8]

我們似乎在租約期長短的問題上陷入了僵局。

---

1 sticking point 癥結；障礙
2 hang up 拖延；耽擱
3 lead time 前置時間（訂貨至交貨所隔的時間）
4 scope [skop] *n.* 範圍
5 outstanding [ˋaʊtˋstændɪŋ] *adj.* 未解決的
6 settle on (sth.) 決定、同意（某事）
7 impasse [ˋɪmpæs] *n.* 死路；僵局
8 duration [dʊˋreʃən] *n.* 期間

52 致力要克服障礙
Committing[1] to Overcoming Sticking Points

☐ Let's not get hung up here. For now, I suggest we agree to disagree on this point, and move forward.

我們不要在這裡被困住了。我建議我們目前先同意大家對這一點的看法不同，然後繼續討論其他的事。

☐ Let's put the issue of distribution aside for the time being, and move on to discuss intellectual property rights.[2]

我們暫時把配銷的議題放在一旁，先討論智慧財產權的問題吧。

☐ We may not see eye to eye[3] on outsourcing,[4] but if we're committed to[5] reaching an agreement, we'll find some common ground.[6]

也許我們對外包的見解不一致，但是如果我們決意要達成協議，我們就會找出一些共同點。

☐ We're determined to[7] resolve this issue in the interest of[8] coming to a fair/workable[9] agreement.

為了達成一項公平／可行的協議，我們下定決心要解決這個問題。

☐ This issue isn't going to go away if we just (continue to) ignore it.

如果我們只是（繼續）忽略這個問題，它是不會消失的。

☐ I'm not going to let one issue derail[10] this deal.

我不會讓一個問題毀掉這項交易。

---

1 commit [kə`mɪt] *v.* 致力；獻身

2 intellectual property rights 智慧財產權

3 see eye to eye 見解完全一致

4 outsource [`aut.sɔrs] *v.* 將商品或服務以合約的方式委外處理

5 be committed to 決意要做……

6 common ground 共同立場；共同點

7 be dertermined to 下定決心要做

8 in the interest of 為了……起見

9 workable [`wɜkəbl] *adj.* 可實行的

10 derail [də`rel] *v.* 使出軌

53 提出替代方案
Introducing Alternatives

☐ We have choices here.
我們是有選擇的。

☐ There is an alternative. / There are several alternatives.
有一個替代方案。／有幾個替代方案。

☐ I'd ask you to consider a cost-sharing[1] arrangement instead.
我想請你們改考慮成本分攤的做法。

☐ Let's consider some of our other options. For instance, we could change the packaging.[2]
我們來考慮一下我們幾個其他的選擇。例如，我們可以改變包裝。

☐ Instead of assembling[3] the chairs in our plant, we could ship them to you unassembled.
我們可以把尚未組裝的椅子運送給你們，而不在我們的工廠裡組裝。

☐ I understand an early January delivery date doesn't work for you,[4] but what about a date closer to the end of the month?
我了解一月初的送貨日期對你們行不通，那接近月底的時候如何呢？

■ cost-sharing 成本分攤
■ packaging [ˋpækɪdʒɪŋ] n. 包裝
■ assemble [əˋsɛmbl̩] v. 組裝
■ work for sb. 對某人而言可以

54 說明某提議的好處
Explaining the Benefits of an Offer

☐ Look at what we're offering you.

看看我們提供給你們的條件。

☐ Offers like this don't come around[1] every day.

這種提議可不是天天都有。

☐ The benefits of our offer (for your company) are obvious/numerous.[2]

我們（給你們公司的）提議的好處非常明顯／極多。

☐ Our offer represents a fantastic[3] opportunity for you (and your organization).

我們的提議對你們（和你們的機構）而言是個絕佳的機會。

☐ Our offer has the benefit of letting you cancel or amend[4] orders on short notice.[5]

我們的提議有讓你們在短時間內取消或修改訂單的好處。

☐ What we're offering not only solves your supply problem in the short term,[6] but also saves you money in the long run.[7]

我們的提議不僅短期內能夠解決你們的供應問題，長期來說還能幫你們省錢。

---

[1] come around 定期發生
[2] numerous [`njumərəs] adj. 很多的
[3] fantastic [fæn`tæstɪk] adj. 【口語】極好的；很棒的
[4] amend [ə`mɛnd] v. 修改
[5] on short notice 在短時間內
[6] in the short term 短期內
[7] in the long run 長期來說

徵詢意見
Soliciting[1] Input

☐ **Do you have anything to add?**
你有任何事情要補充嗎？

☐ **I'd like to know your thoughts on** a copyright agreement.
我想知道你對於達成著作權協議的想法。

☐ **What do you think about** hiring foreign laborers for the project?
你對於為這項專案雇用外籍勞工有何想法？

☐ **What can you tell me about** the market for MP3 players in Malaysia?
關於馬來西亞的 MP3 播放機市場，你有什麼可以告訴我的？

☐ **I'd like some input from you on** how to apportion[2] the liability[3] for the claim.
我想要聽聽你對如何分擔索賠責任的意見。

☐ **Do you have any suggestions as to** how we can get around[4] the import restrictions?[5]
關於我們要如何避開進口管制，你有什麼建議嗎？

---

1 solicit [sə`lɪsɪt] v. 徵求
2 apportion [ə`porʃən] v. 分配；分派；分攤
3 liability [.laɪə`bɪlətɪ] n. 責任；義務
4 get around 避開；克服（困難）

5 restriction [rɪ`strɪkʃən] n. 限制；約束；管制

56

交換條件
Quid Pro Quo[1]

☐ We're willing to meet you halfway[2] on this.

在這一點上，我們願意與你們妥協。

☐ Everybody wants a win-win[3] situation here.

這裡每個人都想達到雙贏的局面。

☐ You scratch my back,[4] and I'll scratch yours.

你幫我，我也幫你。

☐ There's some flexibility[5] on the issue of sales terms.

在銷售條件上有一些彈性。

☐ What can you give/offer us in return for[6] an exclusive distribution deal?

你們可以給予／提供我們什麼來交換獨家經銷的協議？

☐ We're willing to make concessions on the issue of holiday pay in exchange for[7] a union[8] commitment[9] to a wage freeze.[10]

我們願意在假日薪水的議題上讓步，以換取工會承諾凍結薪資。

---

1 quid pro quo [ˌkwɪdproˋkwo] *n.* 交換條件；交換物
2 meet sb. halfway 與某人妥協
3 win-win [ˋwɪnˋwɪn] *adj.* 雙贏的
4 scratch sb.'s back 幫某人抓背（喻幫其忙）
5 flexibility [ˌflɛksəˋbɪlətɪ] *n.* 彈性

6 in return for 作為⋯⋯的交換
7 in exchange for 與⋯⋯交換
8 union [ˋjunjən] *n.* 工會
9 commitment [kəˋmɪtmənt] *n.* 承諾；致力；獻身
10 wage freeze 薪資凍結

Part 7

說服對方
Persuading Your Opponent

57 使用事實和數據
Using Facts and Figures

☐ **The numbers don't lie.**
數字不會說謊。

☐ **You wanted hard[1] numbers; I'm giving you hard numbers.**
你們想要實際的數字,我就給你們實際的數字。

☐ **The numbers confirm/suggest that salaries continue to be our largest expenditure.[2]**
數據證實/顯示薪資仍然是我們最大的支出。

☐ **If you look at the graph/chart, you'll see a sharp[3] drop[4] in sales last month.**
如果你們看這個圖/表,就會看到上個月的銷售量大跌。

☐ **The numbers bear out[5] that demand for flat screens has remained stable in the last three months.**
數據證實平面螢幕的需求在過去三個月來維持穩定。

☐ **Sales figure for the first/second/third/fourth quarter show a nice recovery.[6]**
第一/第二/第三/第四季的銷售數字顯示有不錯的回升。

---

1 hard [hɑrd] *adj.* 可靠的;有具體事實的
2 expenditure [ɪk`spɛndɪtʃə] *n.* 支出
3 sharp [ʃɑrp] *adj.* 急遽的;明顯的
4 drop [drɑp] *n.* 下跌;下降
5 bear out 證實
6 recovery [rɪ`kʌvərɪ] *n.* 恢復;復甦

58 運用時間壓力
Using Time Pressure

這是讓對方同意你的要求的經典手法。你可以說：「Hurry up! I don't have all day.」。但是這有點太直接了，下列的說法比較婉轉、恰當。

☐ **We've got to act now.**
我們必須現在就行動。

☐ **Time is of the essence.**[1]
時間是很寶貴的。

☐ **Time is running out**[2] **on this.**
這件事如今分秒必爭。

☐ **Let's get this done before it's too late.**
我們趕快把它做好，不然就太遲了。

☐ **We can't let this opportunity slip**[3] **away.**
我們不能讓這個機會溜走。

☐ **We've got a very narrow**[4] **window of opportunity**[5] **here.**
我們的契機稍縱即逝。

---

1 of the essence 最重要的
2 run out 耗盡
3 slip [slɪp] *v.* 溜走

4 narrow [`næro] *adj.* 間不容髮的；窄的
5 window of opportunity 時機

59 訴諸理性
Appealing[1] to Reason

☐ Try to see it from our point of view.

試著從我們的觀點來看這件事。

☐ I hope you can understand where I stand.

我希望你可以了解我的立場。

☐ Put yourself in my shoes[2] for a second. What would you do?

站在我的立場想一下。你會怎麼做？

☐ Downsizing[3] makes sense, doesn't it?

精簡人事、減少開支很合理，不是嗎？

☐ What would you do if you were in my position?

如果你站在我的立場，你會怎麼做？

☐ Doing it this way is the right thing to do. Think about it.

這麼做才是正確的做法。好好想一想。

---

1 appeal [əˋpil] *v.* 訴諸（其後與介系詞 to 連用）
2 in sb.'s shoes 站在某人的立場
3 downsizing [ˋdaʊnˏsaɪzɪŋ] *n.* 精簡人事、減少開支

60 使用鼓勵與安撫性用語

MP3 62

Using Encouraging[1] and Conciliatory[2] Language

如果你想要探得更多資訊或是讓對方繼續說話，還可以在下列這些說法後面加上「Please, go on.」。

☐ I hear you.

我聽見你說的了。

☐ I see your point.

我了解你的意思。

☐ I know what you mean.

我知道你是什麼意思。

☐ I hear what you're saying.

我聽到你說的話了。

☐ I see what you're getting at.[3]

我明白你真正的意思。

☐ I understand where you're coming from.

我了解你的論據何在。

---

1 encouraging [ɪnˋkɜɪdʒɪŋ] *adj.* 鼓勵的
2 conciliatory [kənˋsɪlɪəˌtorɪ] *adj.* 安撫的
3 get at 意指；暗示

61 促使對方將概念具像化

Urging[1] an Opponent to Visualize[2] a Concept[3]

☐ Let me paint you a picture. / Picture this, if you will.

讓我幫你畫一幅圖。／如果你願意，請想像這樣的畫面。

☐ Picture a new Center for the Arts in the middle of downtown.

想像在市中心有一座新的藝術中心。

☐ Imagine this: a distribution network stretching[4] across Europe.

想像一下：一個橫跨歐洲的經銷網。

☐ Turn your mind to your ideal office space for a moment.

把你的念頭暫時轉到你理想中的辦公室空間上。

☐ Try to visualize a time when the market was better.

試著想像一下市場轉好時的情景。

☐ When I think of LayZee Fashion Sunglasses, I see good-looking young people playing beach volleyball.

當我想到雷吉時尚太陽眼鏡時，我看到的是帥氣的年輕人在打海灘排球。

---

1 urge [ɝdʒ] *v.* 驅策
2 visualize [ˋvɪʒʊəl͵aɪz] *v.* 使看得見；想像
3 concept [ˋkɑnsɛpt] *n.* 概念
4 stretch [strɛtʃ] *v.* 擴展；延伸

62 提出你的想法
Putting Your Ideas Forward[1]

☐ What we're proposing is a gradual reduction in the workforce.[2]
我們所提議的是漸進式的裁減人力。

☐ We'd like to suggest revising the report to reflect the new findings.
我們想建議重新修改報告以反映出新的發現。

☐ Our idea/plan is to integrate[3] the call center with the customer service department.
我們的主意／計畫是要整合電話客服中心與顧客服務部門。

☐ What we envisage[4] is a mobile phone that combines the features[5] of our best selling models in a futuristic[6] design.
我們所想像的是一支結合我們幾個最暢銷機型之特色的未來手機。

☐ The concept we'd like you to consider is an open-air[7] food court surrounded by swaying[8] palm trees.
我們想要你們考慮的概念是一個有搖曳生姿的棕櫚樹圍繞的露天美食廣場。

☐ We propose to earmark[9] a percentage of the proceeds[10] for research and development.
我們提議將收益的一部分撥出做研發。

---

1 put forward 提出
2 workforce [`wɜk‚fors] n. 勞動力（人口）
3 integrate [`ɪntə‚gret] v. 合併；統一
4 envisage [ɛn`vɪzɪdʒ] v. 想像
5 feature [`fitʃə] n. 特色
6 futuristic [‚fjutʃə`rɪstɪk] adj. 未來的；【口語】

新奇的；新潮的
7 open-air [`opən`ɛr] adj. 露天的；戶外的
8 swaying [`sweɪŋ] adj. 搖擺的
9 earmark [`ɪr‚mɑrk] v. 指定撥款
10 proceeds [`prosidz] n.【複數型】收益

63 要求採取行動
Calling for[1] Action

☐ Someone needs to take charge (of the situation).

必須有人主導（情況）。

☐ We're not afraid to raise the stakes.[2]

我們不怕投入更多。

☐ It all boils down[3] to who's willing to take the initiative.[4]

這歸結起來全取決於誰願意率先採取行動。

☐ It's time to take the bull by the horns[5] and call their bluff.[6]

是挺身面對，要他們亮出底牌的時候了。

☐ We're willing to step up to the plate[7] and make you an offer of sixty-five thousand a month, plus stock options.[8]

我們願意採取行動，一個月給你們六萬五千元，再加上股票選擇權。

☐ Let's up the ante[9] here: a one-time payment of four million for the film rights.

讓我們提高金額：一次付清四百萬元以換取影片播放權。

---

1 call for 要求；需求
2 raise the stakes 投入更多金錢、時間；提高賭金
3 boil down 歸結起來
4 take the initiative 率先（做某事）；主動（做某事）
5 take the bull by the horns 不畏艱難面對挑戰
6 call sb.'s bluff [blʌf] 要求某人亮出底牌
7 step up to the plate 採取行動
8 stock option [ˋstɑk͵ɑpʃən] n. 股票選擇權
9 up the ante [ˋæntɪ] 提高資金；加大賭金

64 指出優點
Pointing Out Benefits

☐ **The beauty of this offer is that** you don't need to quit your other job.
這項提議的妙處在於你不需要辭掉另一份工作。

☐ **This plan is designed to** maximize return[1] on your investment.
這個計畫旨在讓你的投資報酬達到最高。

☐ **What you stand to gain is** exposure[2] to an audience that would otherwise have no opportunity to see your work.
你可能得到的好處就是能在原本沒機會看到你作品的觀眾面前曝光。

☐ **The (main) advantage of this plan/proposal is that** you don't need to put up any money[3] up front.[4]
這項計畫／提議的（主要）好處在於你不需要事先提供任何款項。

☐ **This offer has the (added) benefit of allowing you to** work from home.
這項提議有一個（附加）好處，就是讓你可以在家裏工作。

☐ **The best thing about this deal is that** you can write most of the cost off[5] when it comes to tax time.
這筆交易最棒的地方在於你可以在報稅時將大部分的成本核銷掉。

---

1 return [rɪˋtɜn] *n.* （常用複數型）報酬；獲利
2 exposure [ɪkˋspoʒɚ] *n.* 曝光；曝露
3 put up money 提供（所需的）錢
4 up front 事先地
5 write off 勾銷；注銷

Part **8**

說明你為何未被說服
Explaining Why You Are
Not Persuaded

65 說明你的極限與範圍
Explaining Your Limitations and Parameters[1]

☐ My hands are tied.[2]

我無能為力。

☐ Our margins[3] are very small.

我們的利潤很少。

☐ I'm afraid there's nothing/not much I can do.

我恐怕沒辦法做什麼／做太多。

☐ I have no wiggle[4] room[5] whatsoever[6] on this.

這件事我完全沒有任何調整的空間。

☐ Our costs just don't allow us to go above US$69.00 per[7] barrel.[8]

我們的成本實在不允許我們超過每桶六十九美元。

☐ I have no discretion in the matter. I have to follow company procedure.

我在這件事上沒有裁量權。我必須遵循公司的程序。

---

[1] parameter [pəˋræmətə] n. 界限；範圍
[2] One's hands are tied. 無法施展；無能為力
[3] margin [ˋmardʒɪn] n. 利潤
[4] wiggle [ˋwɪgl] n. 擺動
[5] room [rum] n. 空間
[6] whatsoever [͵hwatsoˋɛvə] adj.（whatever 的強調型）任何的（用於問句和否定句）
[7] per [pɜ] prep. 每
[8] barrel [ˋbærəl] n. 桶

66 當你缺少關鍵資訊時
When You Lack Critical[1] Information

☐ There's still one crucial[2] piece (of information) missing.
還少了一個關鍵（資訊）。

☐ Without sales figures, I simply cannot commit to an order.
沒有銷售數字，我實在不能對訂貨作出承諾。

☐ I can't decide unless you show me last year's balance sheet.[3]
除非你讓我看去年的資產負債表，否則我無法決定。

☐ I'm unable to start the paperwork in the absence of[4] proof of insurance.
沒有保險證明，我不能開始處理文件。

☐ Before I can sign a contract, I need you to give me a copy of the regulations.
我需要你先給我一份法規影本，我才能簽訂合約。

☐ In the absence of a signed and witnessed affidavit[5] from you, there's no way I can process your application.
你沒有給我經簽署且經見證的宣誓書，我不可能處理你的申請。

---

1 critical [ˋkrɪtɪk!] *adj.* 關鍵的；危急的
2 crucial [ˋkruʃəl] *adj.* 決定性的；重要的
3 balance sheet [ˋbæləns.ʃit] *n.* 資產負債表
4 in the absence of 缺乏、沒有……
5 affidavit [.æfəˋdevɪt] *n.* 宣誓書；口供書

67 當你無權決定或採取行動時
When You Lack the Authority[1] to Decide or Act

□ I'll have to run that by Mr. Liu first.
我必須先徵詢劉先生的意見。

□ That goes beyond the scope[2] of my authorization[3]/power.
這超過了我的權責／權力範圍。

□ I'm not authorized[4] to OK an amendment[5] to the contract.
我無權同意合約的修訂。

□ I need to get clearance[6] from the Regional Manager before I can go ahead with the purchase.
我需要得到區域經理的批准，才能進行採購。

□ The board of directors will (ultimately)[7] have the final say[8] on whether or not we can continue construction.
（最終）董事會會有發言權作最後的決議，看營建工程是否可以繼續。

□ I still need to get the green light[9] from head office/the board of directors/the owner/our manager.
我仍然需要得到總公司／董事會／老闆／我們經理的核可。

---

1 authority [ə`θɔrətɪ] *n.* 權力；權威
2 scope [skop] *n.* 範圍
3 authorization [ˌɔθərəˈzeʃən] *n.* 授權
4 authorize [`ɔθəˌraɪz] *v.* 授權

5 amendment [əˈmɛndmənt] *n.* 修正
6 clearance [`klɪrəns] *n.* 批准；許可
7 ultimately [`ʌltəmɪtlɪ] *adv.* 最後；最終
8 have the say 有發言權
9 get the green light 獲得批准、許可

68 指出問題或矛盾
Pointing Out a Problem or Contradiction[1]

☐ There are some obvious contradictions here.
這裡有些明顯的矛盾。

☐ The problem lies in[2] the fact that your numbers don't add up.[3]
問題在於你們的數據說不通。

☐ That doesn't jibe with[4] what I know/I've heard about doing business in Japan.
這和我所知道／聽說在日本做生意的情況並不符合。

☐ The problem, as I see it, is that you haven't given enough thought to[5] market research.
在我看來，問題在於你們沒有好好思考市場調查的事。

☐ My biggest problem with what you've said is your basing your position on anecdotal[6] evidence.
我對於你所說的話最大的異議在於，你的立場是以傳聞證據為基礎。

☐ You're contradicting[7] yourself. First, you said you want to build a Jacuzzi.[8] Now you're saying you want to put in[9] a second garage.
你自相矛盾。一開始你說你想要建造一個按摩浴缸；現在你又說你想加蓋第二個車庫。

---

1 contradiction [ˌkɑntrəˈdɪkʃən] *n.* 否定；矛盾
2 lie in 在於
3 add up 【口語】合道理；說得通
4 jibe [dʒaɪb] with 符合……
5 give thought to 思考、考慮……

6 anecdotal [ˌænɪkˈdotl] *adj.* 軼事的；以傳聞為基礎的
7 contradict [ˌkɑntrəˈdɪkt] *v.* 否定；矛盾
8 Jacuzzi [dʒəˈkuzɪ] *n.* 【商標】按摩浴缸
9 put in 蓋

改變你的立場
Changing Your Position

改變先前的說辭
Backtracking[1] on Something You Said

☐ I'd like to backtrack from what I said earlier.
我想要改變我先前的說辭。

☐ That was a poor choice of words[2] on my part.
我剛剛用字不恰當。

☐ What I said was based on a misunderstanding.
我之前所說的話是因為誤解而造成的。

☐ I'd like to retract[3]/clarify my remarks about our plan to boycott[4] French wine.
我想要收回／澄清我對於我們計畫抵制法國酒的言論。

☐ I shouldn't have said "never." What I should have said is I seldom have occasion[5] to review reports personally.
我不該說「從未」的。我應該說的是我很少有機會親自閱讀報告。

☐ When I said I never set foot[6] anywhere near the property,[7] what I (actually) meant to say was I never set foot on the property itself.
當我說我從未靠近過那塊地皮時，我（實際上）要說的是我從來沒有踏上過那塊地皮。

---

1 backtrack [ˋbæk͵træk] v. 由原路返回；出爾反爾

2 choice of words 用字

3 retract [rɪˋtrækt] v. 收回（說過的話等）

4 boycott [ˋbɔɪ͵kɑt] v. 抵制；杯葛

5 occasion [əˋkeʒən] n. 時機；場合

6 set foot (on) 造訪；踏進

7 property [ˋprɑpətɪ] n. 地產；地皮；財產；資產

70

承認某事
Admitting Something

MP3 72

□ I won't deny that.

我不會否認那個。

□ I'll be the first one to admit that we could've done a better job.

我會是第一個承認我們原本可以做得更好的人。

□ I've never been one to pass the buck.[1]

我從來就不是個會推卸責任的人。

□ I make no bones[2] about what I said (earlier).

我對我（先前）所說的話毫不隱瞞。

□ When I'm wrong, I'm not afraid to come out and say it.

當我犯錯的時候，我不怕站出來說我錯了。

□ I must admit I probably erred[3] when I didn't call Henry Chinaski right away.

我必須承認我沒有馬上打電話給亨利・奇納斯基可能是個錯誤。

Part 9 改變你的立場

---

1 pass the buck　推卸責任
2 make no bones　不隱瞞；坦白承認
3 err [ɝ] v. 犯錯

71 否認某事
Denying Something

☐ Don't put words in my mouth.[1]

不要把我沒說過的話硬塞給我。

☐ I'm not going to be the fall guy[2] here.

我可不打算成為代罪羔羊。

☐ That's not what I said. You (obviously) misunderstood (me).

我不是那麼說的。你（很明顯）誤解（我）了。

☐ It's not fair of you to twist[3] my words/quote[4] me out of context.[5]

你扭曲我的話／對我的話斷章取義很不公平。

☐ Don't blame me (for this). I never had anything to do with the McCree case.

別（拿這件事來）怪我。我跟麥克可里的案子從來就沒有任何關係。

☐ I categorically[6] deny I ever did anything untoward[7] in accepting the bid[8] of Longdong Construction.

我絕對否認在接受龍東建設公司下標這件事上有任何不當的行為。

---

1 put words in sb.'s mouth 硬說某人說過某話

2 fall guy [ˈfɔl‚gaɪ] n. 代罪羔羊

3 twist [twɪst] v. 曲解

4 quote [kwot] v. 引用

5 out of context 斷章取義地

6 categorically [‚kætəˈgɔrɪkl̩ɪ] adv. 絕對地；明確地

7 untoward [ʌnˈtord] adj. 不適宜的

8 bid [bɪd] n. 投標

你被對方說服
You're Convinced by the Other Side

MP3 74

☐ I'm sold.

我被說服了。

☐ You've been very persuasive.[1]

你很有說服力。

☐ You've made a believer out of me.[2]

你讓我全心信服。

☐ I must say I've come around to[3] your way of thinking.

我必須說我已經轉而認同你的想法了。

☐ I've changed my mind based on what you've told me.

基於你告訴我的事情，我已經改變了我的想法。

☐ You've made a convincing[4] case/compelling[5] argument.

你的例證很有說服力／論點讓人信服。

Part 9 改變你的立場

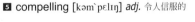

[1] persuasive [pəˋswesɪv] *adj.* 有說服力的
[2] make a believer out of sb. 使某人完全信服
[3] come around to 改變意見轉而贊成
[4] convincing [kənˋvɪnsɪŋ] *adj.* 有說服力的
[5] compelling [kəmˋpɛlɪŋ] *adj.* 令人信服的

Part 10

提議
Offers

73 提議
Making an Offer

MP3 75

最後三個說法可以用來進行假設性的提議,以「試探彼意」。

☐ My offer is/stands at[1] seventy thousand, firm.[2]
我的出價是/就定在七萬元,不會改變。

☐ How does twenty-nine-five (29,500) sound to you?
兩萬九千五你覺得如何?

☐ I'm willing to offer you two million dollars/a three-year contract/exclusive distribution rights.
我願意向你們出價兩百萬元/提供你們一紙三年合約/給你們獨家經銷權。

☐ I'm prepared to offer you forty thousand dollars/ten dollars per kilogram/a one-year license.
我已經準備好要向你們出價四萬元/給你們每公斤十元/提供你們一張一年的執照。

☐ What if I was to offer you a ten percent volume discount[3]/a thirty percent ownership stake[4]/stock options?
如果我提議給你們百分之十的大量訂購折扣/百分之三十的股權/股票選擇權呢?

☐ What would you say to sixty-three cents per unit/a joint partnership/a total order of twelve thousand pieces?
你覺得每一組六毛三/合夥關係/總訂單量一萬兩千件如何?

---

1 stand at 定在……
2 firm [fɝm] *adv.* 堅固地;不變地
3 volume discount [ˋvɑljəmˏdɪskaʊnt] *n.* 因數量大而取得的折扣
4 ownership stake [ˋonəˏʃɪpˏstek] *n.* 股權

74 提出反提議
Making a Counteroffer[1]

☐ How about twenty-eight even[2] (28,000) instead?
改成兩萬八整如何？

☐ I can't do twenty-eight (thousand), but I could do twenty-nine (thousand).
二萬八我沒辦法，但是二萬九可以。

☐ I'll meet you halfway. How about twenty-eight five (28,500)?
我跟你妥協一下。兩萬八千五如何？

☐ I have a counteroffer for you: I can go as high as[3] thirty dollars per unit.
我相對地再提個價錢給你：我最高可以到每一組三十元。

☐ I couldn't take twenty-nine dollars per meter, but I could go as low as[4] thirty.
我沒辦法接受每公尺二十九元，但是我最低可以到三十元。

☐ I'm prepared to raise my offer to eighty-three thousand dollars, but not a penny more.[5]
我已經準備好要把我的出價提高到八萬三千元，但是再多一分錢都不行。

Part 10 提議

---

1 counteroffer [ˋkaʊntə͵ɔfə] *n.* 反提議
2 even [ˋivən] *adj.* 整數的（沒有零頭的）
3 go as high as 最高可以到
4 go as low as 最低可以到
5 not a penny more 多一分錢都不行

有條件地接受提議
Accepting an Offer with Some Qualifications[1]

☐ I'm willing to accept your offer, provisionally.[2]
我願意暫且接受你的提議。

☐ I accept, provided[3] that you agree to drop the lawsuit.
如果你同意放棄法律訴訟，我就接受。

☐ There's one/a couple of prerequisite(s)[4] to our accepting your offer.
要我們接受你們的提議，有一個／幾個前提。

☐ I can accept your offer on one condition[5]/on the following condition: You agree not to lay off[6] any employees for one year.
我可以接受你的提議，但是有一個條件／有下面的條件：你同意在一年內不遣散任何員工。

☐ Our acceptance is conditional[7] upon you making a written apology in the major daily papers.
要我們接受是有條件的，你得在各大日報上刊登書面道歉啟示。

☐ So long as you guarantee[8] you will pay the royalties[9] owed to Mr. Mason and myself, I accept your offer.
只要你保證會給付積欠梅森先生和我的版稅，我就接受你的提議。

---

1 qualification [ˌkwɑləfəˋkeʃən] *n.* 限定性條件
2 provisionally [prəˋvɪʒənḷɪ] *adv.* 暫時地；臨時地
3 provided [prəˋvaɪdɪd] *conj.* 在……條件下；如果
4 prerequisite [ˌpriˋrɛkwəzɪt] *n.* 先決條件；必要條件
5 on one condition 有一個條件
6 lay off 解雇
7 conditional [kənˋdɪʃənḷ] *adj.* 附有條件的
8 guarantee [ˌgærənˋti] *v.* 保證
9 royalty [ˋrɔɪəltɪ] *n.* 版稅

76 接受提議
Accepting an Offer

☐ I accept.

我接受。

☐ It's a deal.[1]

就這麼說定了。

☐ We can agree to those terms.

我們可以同意那些條件。

☐ I'm satisfied. We have an agreement.

我很滿意。我們達成了共識。

☐ Looks like we've got ourselves a deal.

看來我們達成協議了。

☐ Those terms are agreeable[2]/satisfactory to me.

那些條件我同意/我覺得很滿意。

Part
10
提議

---

1 It's a deal. 就這麼說定了；成交
2 agreeable [ə`griəbl] *adj.* 可以同意的

拒絕提議
Rejecting an Offer

在這些說法的前面都可以加上「Sorry, ...」。或者，如果你沒什麼好損失的，提議又十分不合理，你也可以先說：「Are you crazy?」

☐ Sorry. No deal.

抱歉。不成。

☐ I'm afraid I can't do that.

我恐怕不能那樣做。

☐ I can't accept that offer.

我不能接受那個提議。

☐ I have to reject your offer.

我必須拒絕你的提議。

☐ I can't agree to those terms.

我不能同意那些條件。

☐ Is that the best you can do?

你最多就只能那樣了嗎？

78 有條件地拒絕提議
Rejecting an Offer with Some Qualifications

☐ If you could cut us a little slack[1] on the deadline, we could accept.
如果你們在期限上可以通融一下，我們就能接受。

☐ We're almost there, but we need you to agree to a handling fee.
我們就快達成共識了，但是我們需要你們同意給付手續費。

☐ We'd be willing to accept if you could drop your price by another dollar.
如果你們可以再降價一元，我們就願意接受。

☐ We can't accept twelve-five (12,500), but if you could go to twelve-seven (12,700), we'd be in business.
我們無法接受一萬兩千五，但是如果你可以提高到一萬兩千七，我們就可以成交。

☐ The only thing preventing us from accepting is your insistence on top-billing. [2]
唯一一件讓我們無法接受的事情就是你堅持要把你的名字擺在最前面。

☐ I'm saying no, but I'm leaving the door open[3] to you submitting[4] a revised proposal that meets with the guidelines.
我現在拒絕，但是我會給你機會再遞上一份修改過並符合指導方針的提議書。

---

[1] cut sb. a little slack 通融一下
[2] top-billing [ˈtɑpˈbɪlɪŋ] *n.* 名字擺最前面
[3] leave the door open 給予機會
[4] submit [səbˈmɪt] *v.* 提出

表達情緒
Expressing Emotions

79 對進展表示興奮
Expressing Excitement over Progress Made

☐ We've resolved a lot of issues today.

我們今天解決了很多議題。

☐ I'm encouraged by what we've accomplished[1] thus far.[2]

我對我們目前為止所達成的目標感到鼓舞。

☐ Things are going very well so far. I hope we can keep it up.[3]

到目前為止一切都進行得非常順利。我希望我們可以保持下去。

☐ I think it's fair to say we've made some excellent headway.[4]

我認為持平而論我們已有非常好的進展。

☐ I'd say we're well on our way to a deal/resolution[5]/compromise.[6]

我認為我們在達成協議／找出解決方案／達成妥協上大有進展。

☐ It's nice/great that both sides are so determined to reach an agreement.

雙方都如此決意要達成共識是件不錯／很棒的事。

---

1 accomplish [əˋkɑmplɪʃ] v. 完成
2 thus far 至今
3 keep it up 保持（好的狀況）
4 make headway 進展；前進

5 resolution [ˌrɛzəˋluʃən] n. 解決
6 compromise [ˋkɑmprəˌmaɪz] n. 妥協；折衷方案

80 對缺乏進展表達挫折感
Expressing Frustration[1] over Lack of Progress

☐ A lot of issues are still unresolved.[2]

還有許多議題都尚未解決。

☐ We'll never get anything done at this rate![3]

依照這種速度，我們永遠都完成不了任何事！

☐ I'm not encouraged by what's transpired[4] so far.

我對目前為止的進展並不感到振奮。

☐ I think we're off to a bad/slow/shaky[5] start[6] here.

我認為我們一開頭就不順／速度緩慢／不穩固。

☐ We seem to be getting bogged down[7] in the details.

我們似乎被細節困住了。

☐ Things are going much more slowly than we anticipated.[8]

事情的發展比我們預期的要慢得多。

Part
11
表達情緒

---

1 frustration [frʌs`treʃən] *n.* 挫折
2 unresolved [ˌʌnrɪ`zɑlvd] *adj.* 未解決的
3 at this rate　照這種速度；照這種情形
4 transpire [træn`spaɪr] *v.*【口語】（事情等）
　　發生
5 shaky [`ʃekɪ] *adj.* 不安定的；不穩固的
6 be off to a ... start　一開始就……
7 get bogged [bɑgd] down　陷入泥沼；動彈
　　不得
8 anticipate [æn`tɪsəˌpet] *v.* 期待；預期

81 對提議表示滿意
Expressing Satisfaction with a Proposal

☐ Your proposal gives us a lot to think about.
你的提議讓我們有許多要思考的。

☐ The merits[1] of such a proposal are easy to see.
這樣一項提議的好處是顯而易見的。

☐ Your proposal goes a long way towards[2] bridging the gap[3] between our organizations.
你的提議對於減少我們機構之間的隔閡大有助益。

☐ Your proposal reflects a thoughtful analysis of the socio-economic[4] factors that underlie[5] this conflict.[6]
你的提議反映出對於這個衝突背後的社經因素有深思熟慮的分析。

☐ I (especially) like the fact that your proposal takes environmental factors into account.[7]
我（特別）喜歡的是你的提議確實將環境因素納入了考量。

☐ I appreciate all the hard work that obviously went into such a well-written proposal.
我很欣賞在這份寫得很棒的提議背後明顯付出的努力。

---

1 merit [ˋmɛrɪt] *n.* 優點；好處
2 go a long way towards 對……大有用處
3 bridge the gap 填補縫隙；彌合差距
4 socio-economic [ˋsosɪoˏikəˋnɑmɪk] *adj.* 社會經濟的
5 underlie [ˏʌndəˋlaɪ] *v.* 成為……的基礎；潛存於……之下
6 conflict [ˋkɑnflɪkt] *n.* 衝突
7 take sth. into account 把……納入考量

對提議表示不滿
Expressing Dissatisfaction with a Proposal

☐ Your proposal falls well short of[1] offering a realistic[2] compromise.
你的提議離提出切合實際的折衷方案還差了一大截。

☐ Several aspects of your proposal seem rather unrealistic/ simplistic.[3]
你提議裏的幾個面向似乎都滿不切實際／簡略的。

☐ This proposal strikes me as[4] a rather poor attempt[5] to gloss[6] over the real issues.
這項提議讓我覺得是很彆腳地試圖要粉飾真正的問題。

☐ What you propose fails to take into account the fickle[7] nature of the consumers in the target demographic.[8]
你的提議未能將目標人口中顧客群的善變特性納入考量。

☐ Your proposal doesn't even begin to address[9] the problems you've been having with making deliveries on time.
你的提議根本沒有針對你們一直無法準時交貨的問題提出解決方案。

☐ I must point out to you that this proposal has several obvious shortcomings,[10] as far as we're concerned.
我必須向你指出，在我們看來這項提議有幾個明顯的缺失。

---

1 fall short of 未達；不足
2 realistic [ˌrɪəˋlɪstɪk] *adj.* 切合實際的
3 simplistic [sɪmˋplɪstɪk] *adj.* 過份簡化的
4 strike sb. as 讓某人覺得是⋯⋯；給某人⋯⋯的印象
5 attempt [əˋtɛmpt] *n.* 嘗試；企圖

6 gloss [glɔs] *v.* 掩飾（其後用介系詞 over）
7 fickle [ˋfɪkl] *adj.* 易變的；善變的
8 demographic [ˌdɛməˋgræfɪk] *n.* 部分族群
9 address [əˋdrɛs] *v.* 處理（問題等）
10 shortcoming [ˋʃɔrt.kʌmɪŋ] *n.* 短處；缺點

Part *11* 表達情緒

83 放慢步調
Slowing the Pace

MP3 85

☐ Let's not get ahead of ourselves.[1]
我們別操之過急。

☐ Let's just slow down for a minute.
我們就先放慢一下。

☐ First things first.[2] Let's not be hasty.[3]
該做的先做。我們不要躁進。

☐ Let's take things one step at a time.
我們一步一步來。

☐ Slow down! Let's not rush into things.[4]
慢一點！我們不要倉促行事。

☐ We can't put the cart before the horse.[5]
我們不能本末倒置。

---

[1] get ahead of oneself 操之過急
[2] First things first. 該做的先做。
[3] hasty [ˋhestɪ] *adj.* 匆忙的

[4] rush into things 倉促行事
[5] put the cart before the horse 本末倒置

84 表達急切感
Expressing Urgency

☐ We're wasting time.
我們在浪費時間。

☐ The clock's ticking[1] on this.
這件事現在是分秒必爭。

☐ I have to leave in an hour.
我必須一個小時後離開。

☐ I don't have any time to waste.
我沒有任何時間可以浪費。

☐ I'm not leaving here without a deal.
沒有達成協議，我不會離開這裡。

☐ It's imperative[2] that we get something on paper[3] today.
我們今天一定要達成某些書面協議。

Part
11
表
達
情
緒

---

[1] tick [tɪk] *v.* (鐘錶等) 滴答響 (**the clock is ticking** 指時間一分一秒地過去，所剩不多)
[2] imperative [ɪm`pɛrətɪv] *adj.* 必要的；非做不可的
[3] on paper 書面上

Part **12**

改變氣氛
Changing the Mood

85 保持專注與正面態度
Staying Focused and Positive

☐ There's no point in bickering.[1]

鬥嘴無益。

☐ Let's not lose sight of[2] our objective.

我們不要忘了我們的目標是什麼。

☐ I'd like to keep the tone[3] of this meeting friendly.

我想要讓這場會議的氣氛保持融洽。

☐ Everyone looks so serious. Let's lighten up[4] a little.

大家看起來好嚴肅。我們放輕鬆一點。

☐ You look upset/concerned/unhappy. What's troubling you?

你看起來不太高興／有些擔心／不太開心。你在煩心什麼？

☐ Let's remember that what we're here to do is to avert[5] a disruption[6] in the production schedule.

大家要記住，我們到這裡來要做的事是避免生產時程表出現中斷。

---

[1] bickering [ˋbɪkərɪŋ] *n.* 爭論
[2] lose sight of 忘記；忽略
[3] tone [ton] *n.* 氣氛；語氣
[4] lighten up 輕鬆一點；高興起來
[5] avert [əˋvɝt] *v.* 防止；避免
[6] disruption [dɪsˋrʌpʃən] *n.* 中斷；混亂

86 緩和你的言辭
Toning Down[1] Your Language

如果你說了什麼讓人倒抽一口氣或是感到震驚的話，趕快接著說下列的其中一句吧。

☐ Let me put it another way.
讓我換個方式來說。

☐ That was a poor choice of words on my part.
我剛剛的選辭用字很不恰當。

☐ Please, don't take offense[2]/don't take it personally.[3]
請不要見怪／不要覺得這是人身攻擊。

☐ I hope you won't misconstrue[4] my words/meaning.
我希望你沒有誤會我的話／意思。

☐ I didn't mean to offend[5] (you). Let me rephrase[6] that ....
我不是有意要冒犯（你）。讓我換個說法……。

☐ Perhaps my words were a little strong/insensitive[7]/blunt.[8]
也許我的用字有點強烈／沒有顧慮別人的感受／唐突。

Part 12 改變氣氛

---

1 tone down 緩和
2 take offense [ə`fɛns] 對……不悅
3 take it personally 認為是人身攻擊
4 misconstrue [`mɪskən,stru] v. 誤會
5 offend [ə`fɛnd] v. 冒犯

6 rephrase [ri`frez] v. 改變措辭來表達
7 insensitive [ɪn`sɛnsətɪv] adj. 不顧及別人感受的
8 blunt [blʌnt] adj. 直言不諱的

87 讓情勢加溫
Escalating[1]

當談判氣氛變得激烈，下列這些說法不管是用來提出威脅或反將對方一軍都蠻好用的。

☐ Is that a threat?

那是威脅嗎？

☐ Am I supposed to be intimidated?[2]

我應該被嚇得皮皮挫嗎？

☐ Oh yeah? Do I look worried/scared?

噢，是嗎？我看起來像是很擔心／很害怕的樣子嗎？

☐ I hope that's not (meant as) a threat.

我希望那不是威脅（的意思）。

☐ Are you trying to make me angry? You wouldn't like me when I'm angry.

你是想讓我發火嗎？你不會喜歡我發火的樣子的。

☐ I didn't want to stoop[3] to that level, but if you want to take it there, I can give as good as I get.[4]

我不想降格到那個層次，但是如果你想那樣玩，我可不會輸給你。

---

1 escalate [`ɛskə͵let] *v.* 逐步上升
2 intimidate [ɪn`tɪmə͵det] *v.* 恫嚇
3 stoop [stup] *v.* 降格
4 I can give as good as I get. 我可不會輸給你。

88 讓情勢降溫
De-escalating[1]

當大家情緒火爆時，可使用以下這些說法來避免情勢失控。

☐ There's no point[2] going off half-cocked.[3]
輕率衝動沒有意義。

☐ Let's try to maintain some decorum[4] here.
大家還是試著保持一些禮貌吧。

☐ Let's attack points, not the people making them.
大家就事論事，不要作人身攻擊。

☐ Let's take a few minutes so everybody can cool off.[5]
我們休息幾分鐘，讓每個人都能冷靜一下。

☐ I think we all need to calm down. I suggest we take a break and get some fresh air.
我認為我們都需要冷靜下來。我建議我們休息一下，呼吸一些新鮮空氣。

☐ I know you're a reasonable person. In fact, we're all reasonable people.
我知道你是一個講道理的人。事實上，我們都是講道理的人。

Part 12 改變氣氛

---

1 de-escalate [di`ɛskə͵let] *v.* 逐步降低
2 point [pɔɪnt] *n.* 用處；意義
3 half-cocked [`hæf͵kɑkt] *adj.* 準備不周的；輕率行動的
4 decorum [dɪ`korəm] *n.* 禮節；禮儀
5 cool off 使冷卻；使平息

Part **13**

會議控制與流程
Meeting Control and Flow

89 發言
Taking the Floor[1]

- [ ] I'll be brief.
  我會長話短說。

- [ ] I'll get right to the point.[2]
  我會直接說重點。

- [ ] I have a lot to say. I'll ask you to bear with[3] me.
  我有許多要說的。請大家多擔待。

- [ ] Before I begin, I'd like to say I'm glad to finally have the chance to meet with all of you.
  在我開始之前,我想說我很高興終於有機會能夠和你們大家見面。

- [ ] I'd like to start off[4] by mentioning that everything said today is to be held in strictest confidence.[5]
  一開始,我想先提一下,今天我們說的所有話都要視為最高機密。

- [ ] I should preface[6] my remarks[7] by saying that I'm most impressed by what I saw on the tour of your plant.
  我在正式說話之前,應該先提一下,我在參觀你們工廠時,對於所見印象極為深刻。

---

1 take the floor 發言;參與討論
2 get to the point 說出重點
3 bear with 忍耐;忍受
4 start off 開始(做某事)

5 hold in confidence [`kɑnfədəns] 視為機密
6 preface [`prɛfɪs] v. 以……為講話(文章)的開端
7 remark [rɪ`mɑrk] n. 話;評論

90 打斷別人談話
Interrupting[1]

☐ Excuse me.
對不起。

☐ Sorry to cut you off,[2] but I have a very relevant point to make.
抱歉打斷你的話，但是我有一個非常相關的要點要提出來。

☐ I hate to interrupt (you), but what you just said isn't quite right.
我很不願意打斷（你），但是你剛說的不是很正確。

☐ Pardon me for interrupting, but there is something I should say before we go any further.
請原諒我打斷，但是在我們繼續談下去之前，有件事我必須說。

☐ Excuse/Forgive/Pardon the interruption, but your PowerPoint slide is upside down.[3]
請原諒我打斷，但是你的 PowerPoint 投影片放反了。

☐ Please, continue with what you were saying.
麻煩你繼續剛才所說的話。

---

1 interrupt [ˌɪntəˈrʌpt] v. 打斷談話
2 cut off 中斷；切斷
3 upside down 顛倒

91 應付別人的打斷
Dealing with Interruptions

☐ Please, let me finish.
麻煩,請讓我說完。

☐ Did you have a question?
你有問題嗎?

☐ Yes, what's your question?
是的,你有什麼問題?

☐ That's a good/fair question.
那是個好/合理的問題。

☐ I'd ask you to hold your questions until I conclude my remarks.
我要請你把問題留到我說完話之後再問。

☐ I let you have your say,[1] and now I'd appreciate the same courtesy.[2]
我讓你表達了你的意見,現在如果能得到相同的禮遇我會很感激。

---

1 have one's say 有機會發表意見
2 courtesy [ˋkɝtəsɪ] *n.* 禮貌

92 在被打斷後重回論點
Returning to a Point After an Interruption

☐ **As I was saying,** the proposal has not yet been approved by the manager.

正如我剛才說的，這提案還未得到經理的認可。

☐ **Now, where was I?** Oh yes, if you look at these figures, you'll see this is a great deal.

好，我剛才說到哪兒？喔，對了，如果你看看這些數據，就會明白這是筆大交易。

☐ **The point I was trying to make is** our board[1] won't approve a contract that isn't recognized as valid by the EU.[2]

我剛才試著要說明的是，我們的董事會不會通過不被歐盟認為有效的合約。

☐ **To get back to what I was saying,** we really need better numbers before we decide.

回到我剛才所說的，我們在決定之前真的需要一些更好的數據。

☐ **To continue/pick up where I left off,**[3] the contract needs a boilerplate clause[4] before I can sign it.

繼續／重回我剛才說了一半的話，合約一定要有標準條款我才能簽。

☐ **To return to/finish my (original) point,** we can only provide half the content[5]—no more no less.

回到／繼續說完我（原本）的話，我們只能提供一半的內容——不多也不少。

---

1 board [bord] *n.* 董事會

2 EU 歐盟（European Union 的縮寫）

3 pick up where one leaves off 從某人停頓的地方重新開始

4 boilerplate clause [ˋbɔɪlɚ͵plet`klɔz] *n.* 標準條款

5 content [ˋkɑntənt] *n.* 內容

特定的談判議題
Specific Negotiation Issues

Part 1

金錢
Money

93 要求對方開出價碼
Asking Your Opponent to Name Their Price

☐ Name your price.[1]

開出你的價碼吧。

☐ What's your bottom line?[2]

你們的底限是多少錢？

☐ And your asking price is ...?

你們要求的價格是……？

☐ How much is this going to cost me?

這會花我多少錢？

☐ How much are you prepared to offer?

你們準備要出價多少？

☐ What are we talking about here in dollars and cents?

我們現下談論的到底是多少錢？

---

1 name one's price　開出價碼
2 bottom line　底限

94 開出你的價碼
Stating Your Price

☐ **The best price we can offer you is** eighty cents per roll.

我們能提給你的最好價格是每捲八十分。

☐ **The unit price per memory card[1] is** seven hundred fifty NT.

每張記憶卡的單位價格是新台幣七百五十元。

☐ **We charge** seven ninety-five ($7.95) **per** five liter[2] container.[3]

我們每五公升裝的要價七點九五美元。

☐ **Our prices are based on/fluctuate[4] with** order volume.

我們的價格是依訂量而定／而有所變動。

☐ **I can take** twenty three thousand, **but not a penny less.**

我可以接受兩萬三千元，但是一分錢都不能少。

☐ **We can offer to sell you our** 40-watt[5] bulbs[6] **at a special price of** seventeen cents each.

我們可以以每個十七分的特價將我們四十瓦的燈泡賣給你們。

---

1 memory card [ˈmɛmərɪ͵kɑrd] *n.* 記憶卡
2 liter [ˈlitə] *n.* 公升
3 container [kənˈtenə] *n.* 容器
4 fluctuate [ˈflʌktʃu͵et] *v.* 波動；變動

5 watt [wɑt] *n.* 瓦特
6 bulb [bʌlb] *n.* 電燈泡

95 價格過高
The Price is Too High

☐ That's a little steep,[1] isn't it?

這有點太貴了，不是嗎？

☐ Sorry. That's too rich for my blood.[2]

抱歉。這對我來說太貴了。

☐ I'm afraid we (just) can't go that high.

恐怕我們（實在）沒辦法接受那麼高的價格。

☐ That's (way)[3] beyond our means[4]/budget.[5]

那（遠）超出我們的財力／預算。

☐ That's (a lot) more than your competitors charge.

這比你們競爭對手的要價要高（許多）。

☐ I have to tell you that figure isn't even in the ballpark.[6]

我得告訴你，那個數字完全不在可接受的範圍內。

---

1 steep [stip] *adj.* 過高的；不合理的
2 too rich for one's blood 對某人而言太貴了
3 way [we] *adv.* 遠遠地；大大地
4 means [minz] *n.* 財產；財富
5 budget [ˋbʌdʒɪt] *n.* 預算
6 in the ballpark 在正確的範圍之內

96 出價太低
The Offer is Too Low

☐ Is that the best you can do?

你最多只能出這個價錢了嗎？

☐ That's quite a bit[1] lower than we expected.

這比我們原來預期的低了不少。

☐ Surely you can do a little better than that.

你們一定可以出比這更好一點的價錢。

☐ That's impossible, I'm afraid. Our margins[2] are very small.

恐怕那是不可能的。我們的毛利很少。

☐ If we sold (to you) at that price, we'd stand to take a loss.

如果我們以那個價錢賣出（給你們），我們可能會虧錢。

☐ At that price we wouldn't even / would barely be covering our costs.

以那個價錢我們甚至不能／幾乎不夠支付我們的成本。

---

1 quite a bit 不少
2 margin [`mɑrdʒɪn] *n.* 毛利；利潤

97 要求折扣
Asking for a Discount

☐ Can you give us a discount?
你們可不可以給我們打個折？

☐ What would it take for you to discount the price?
你們要怎麼樣才會打折？

☐ We hope you'll agree to a discount based on the size of our order.
我們希望你們會依據我們的訂單量同意打個折。

☐ We typically receive a volume discount of between three and five percent from our other suppliers.
我們其他的供應商通常都會給我們百分之三到五的大量訂購折扣。

☐ Could you knock a little off[1] the price, say three cents per unit, if we take more than seventy thousand per shipment?[2]
如果我們每批貨訂七萬個以上，你們可不可以稍微降點價，比方說每個少三分？

☐ If you could offer us a (volume) discount, we could guarantee a monthly/quarterly[3] order of ten thousand dishware sets.[4]
如果你們可以給我們（大量訂購）折扣，我們可以保證每月／每季訂購一萬套餐具。

---

1 knock off 【口語】減價
2 shipment [ˈʃɪpmənt] *n.* 一批貨；裝運
3 quarterly [ˈkwɔrtəlɪ] *adj.* 按季的
4 dishware set [ˈdɪʃ.wɛr.sɛt] *n.* （盛食物的）餐具組

98 回應折扣的請求或提供折扣 MP3 100

Responding to a Request for a Discount or Offering a Discount

回應折扣要求

□ I can't do six percent, but how about five?
百分之六我沒辦法，但是百分之五如何？

□ Sorry, we can't give a discount on an order of that size.
抱歉，這種數量的訂單我們沒辦法打折。

□ We can probably knock five percent off the price of the order.
我們大概可以把那張訂單的價格降低個百分之五。

□ We could agree to a discount in that amount if you could guarantee a minimum[1] monthly order of two thousand pieces.
如果你們可以保證每個月最少訂購兩千件，我們就可以同意提供那樣的折扣。

提供折扣

□ We're willing to cut our price by two percent as a special discount for you.
我們願意降價百分之二，當作是給你們的特別折扣。

□ As an added incentive,[2] I'm prepared to offer you a discount of ten percent.
我已經準備好要給你們百分之十的折扣，當作是附加報酬。

---

1 minimum [ˈmɪnəməm] *n.* 最小限額
2 incentive [ɪnˈsɛntɪv] *n.* 誘因；獎勵；報酬

99 付款條件與方式
Payment Terms and Methods

☐ How do you plan to pay?

你打算要如何付款？

☐ We'd prefer payment by bank draft.[1]

我們比較喜歡以銀行匯票付款。

☐ Do you accept payment by credit card?

你們接受以信用卡付款嗎？

☐ We have to insist on payment by letter of credit.[2]

我們必須堅持以信用狀付款。

☐ Our policy is that accounts are payable[3] (in full[4]) within thirty days of receipt of each shipment.

我們的政策是在收到每批貨的三十天內應支付（全額）帳款。

☐ Certified cheque[5] and bank draft are the only two methods of payment we accept.

我們只接受兩種付款方式：保付支票和銀行匯票。

---

1 bank draft [ˋbæŋk͵dræft] *n.* 銀行匯票
2 letter of credit [ˋlɛtəˈɝˋkrɛdɪt] *n.* 信用狀
3 payable [ˋpeəbl] *adj.* 應付的
4 in full 全額

5 certified cheque [ˋsɝtə͵faɪdˋtʃɛk] *n.* 保付支票

100 銷售條件
Sales Terms

☐ All sales are final.
商品售出，概不退換。

☐ We have to insist that all sales are F.O.B., Keelung.
我們必須堅持所有的商品交易都是基隆起運的船上交貨價格。

☐ We'd be much more comfortable if the sales terms could be D.D.P.,[1] Brisbane.
如果銷售條件是在布里斯本完稅後交貨，我們會覺得比較舒坦一些。

☐ As seller, we'd be responsible for freight[2] and insurance charges as far as the port of Hualien.
身為賣方，我們會負擔到花蓮港之前的運費和保險費。

☐ Our products are guaranteed against defects[3] in materials and workmanship[4] for a period of one year.
我們的產品有一年材料和做工缺陷的保固期。

☐ As the buyer, you'd be responsible for picking up the goods and transporting them from the wharf[5] to your facilities.
身為買家，你們要負責接收貨物並將它們從碼頭運送到你們的工廠。

---

1 D.D.P. 完稅後交貨（Delivered Duty Paid 的縮寫）
2 freight [fret] *n.* 運費
3 defect [dɪˋfɛkt] *n.* 缺陷；瑕疵
4 workmanship [ˋwɝkmənˌʃɪp] *n.* 做工；手藝
5 wharf [hwɔrf] *n.* 碼頭

Part **2**

....

時間
Time

101 重要時間點與期限
Milestones[1] and Deadlines

建議

☐ Why don't we set June 30 as the date for the grand opening?
我們何不把六月三十日訂為盛大開幕日？

☐ We need to choose a date for completion of the manuscript.[2]
How about December fifteenth?
我們需要選一天作為完稿日。十二月十五日如何？

☐ How does August 31 sound to you as the cutoff[3] date for
receiving applications?[4]
你覺得把八月三十一日當成申請受理截止日如何？

☐ We should look to have the contract drawn up[5] in final form by
September first.
我們應該要想辦法在九月一日前擬定最終版本的合約。

回應

☐ That's too soon. We/It/They won't be ready/finished.
那樣太快了。我們／東西／他們沒辦法準備好／完成的。

☐ That's too late. We'll miss the holiday travel season/the big sale.
那樣太晚了。我們會錯過假日旅遊季／大拍賣。

---

1 milestone [ˋmaɪl.ston] *n.* 里程碑；重大事件
2 manuscript [ˋmænjə.skrɪpt] *n.* 原稿
3 cutoff [ˋkʌt.ɔf] *n.* 切斷；截止
4 application [.æpləˋkeʃən] *n.* 申請
5 draw up 擬（合約）

生產時程
Production Schedules

☐ We can provide three thousand **units** per month.
我們每個月可以提供三千組。

☐ We need these products by November tenth **at the very latest**.[1]
我們最遲需要在十一月十日拿到這些產品。

☐ Can you **fill**[2] an order for two hundred lab **kits**[3] by June twenty-first?
你們可以在六月二十一日前提供兩百套實驗室用品組嗎?

☐ We can alter the production schedule to give you time to re-tool.[4]
我們可以更改生產時程好讓你們有時間更換機具。

☐ We (don't) have the **capacity**[5] to **turn out**[6] two hundred and fifty motors by the end of next month.
我們的產能(不)足以在下個月月底前生產出兩百五十具馬達。

☐ We can **build flexibility into**[7] the production schedule to allow for seasonal **fluctuations**[8] in demand.
我們可以在生產時程中加入一些彈性以配合季節性的需求波動。

---

[1] at the (very) latest 最遲
[2] fill an order 供應訂貨
[3] kit [kɪt] *n.* 一組工具
[4] re-tool [ri`tul] *v.* 更換(工廠的)機器

[5] capacity [kə`pæsətɪ] *n.* (工廠等的)生產力
[6] turn out 生產;製造
[7] build into 使成為(……的)一部分
[8] fluctuation [ˌflʌktʃʊ`eʃən] *n.* 波動

我們需要更多時間
We Need More Time

☐ Can you give us more time?

你們能不能給我們更多時間？

☐ Could we make it for a later date?

我們可不可以晚幾天？

☐ We're (a little/way) behind schedule.[1]

我們的進度（有一點／大大）落後。

☐ We'd appreciate it if you could give us a bit of breathing room.[2]

如果你們可以給我們一點喘息的機會，我們會很感激。

☐ Can we push the date for delivery back a bit, to say ... October eleventh?

我們能不能把送貨日期往後延一點，比如說十月十一日？

☐ It doesn't look like we're going to be able to meet the deadline for filing a claim.[3]

看來我們好像沒辦法趕上申請索賠的期限。

---

[1] behind schedule　比預定的進度慢
[2] breathing room　喘息的機會
[3] file a claim　申請索賠

104

我們可以完成
We Can Do It

當對方問你:「Can you make it?」時,你可以用下列的說法來肯定地回應,或是積極地說服對方你可以處理這個案子。

☐ We've made this a top priority.

我們已經把這件事當成最優先事項。

☐ We're working around the clock[1] to fill this order.

我們現在一天做二十四小時以應付這張訂單的需求。

☐ We've redoubled[2] our efforts to make up for lost time.

我們已經加倍努力來彌補損失掉的時間。

☐ I have no doubt we'll finish on time/ahead of schedule.[3]

我認為我們必定會準時/提前完成。

☐ We've got three shifts[4]/our people working on the project, 24-7.[5]

我們有三班的人/我們的人一天二十四小時、一週七天在做這項計畫。

☐ If we put our noses to the grindstone,[6] I know we can still come in on time/on budget.[7]

如果我們不眠不休,我知道我們還是可以準時/在預算內完成。

---

[1] around the clock 二十四小時連續不斷地
[2] redouble [ri`dʌbl] v. 使……再倍增
[3] ahead of schedule 比預定的時間早
[4] shift [ʃɪft] n. 輪班
[5] 24-7 一天二十四小時、一週七天地

[6] grindstone [`graɪnd.ston] n. 磨石(put sb.'s nose to the grindstone 指使某人勤奮工作;使某人埋頭苦幹)
[7] on budget 在預算內

Part3

裝貨、運送與倉儲
Shipment, Delivery, and Storage

105 裝運
Shipping

☐ How will the products be shipped to Amsterdam?
產品會如何運送到阿姆斯特丹？

☐ The fruit needs to be protected against spoilage[1] during transport.
水果在運送過程中需要受到保護，以免損壞。

☐ We need to discuss the apportionment[2] of shipping costs between us.
我們需要討論我們之間運送成本的分攤比例。

☐ What kind of arrangements are in place[3] for shipping the merchandise/products/consignments?[4]
運送商品／產品／託售貨品有什麼樣適當的安排？

☐ The products will be shipped by container ship[5] to Montreal. From there, they will be transported to Toronto by truck.
產品會由貨櫃船運送到蒙特婁。從那兒，它們會再被用卡車載到多倫多。

☐ The consignment(s) must be delivered to Mr. Azul at Azul's Restaurant in New York.
託售貨品必須送交給紐約阿祖爾餐廳的阿祖爾先生。

---

1 spoilage [`spɔɪlɪdʒ] n. 損壞
2 apportionment [ə`porʃənmənt] n. 分配；分攤
3 in place 適當的
4 consignment [kən`saɪnmənt] n. 委託的貨物；託售的貨品
5 container ship [kən`tenɚ.ʃɪp] n. 貨櫃船

106 倉儲
Storage[1]

MP3 108

☐ Could you give me a list of your storage/shipping tariffs?[2]
你可不可以給我一張你們倉儲／貨運的價目表？

☐ We require that the storage facility be secure and climate[3] controlled.
我們要求倉庫必須安全而且有空調管控。

☐ The wharfage[4] fees should work out to[5] about two thousand pounds (£ 2000).
碼頭使用費合計應達兩千鎊左右。

☐ We need to store a quantity of riding lawnmowers[6] for a period of thirty days.
我們需要儲存三十天量的乘坐式割草機。

☐ Is your warehouse able to accommodate[7] three thousand boxes of fabric softener?[8]
你們的倉庫能夠存放三千箱的衣物柔軟精嗎？

☐ We can't take delivery[9] until the end of the month.
我們要到月底才能收貨。

☐ We'd like to keep the samples at your facility until then, if we may.
如果可以的話，在那之前我們想把樣本存放在你們的倉庫裡。

---

1 storage [`storɪdʒ] *n.* 貯藏；保管
2 tariff [`tærɪf] *n.* 收費表；價目表
3 climate [`klaɪmɪt] *n.* 氣候
4 wharfage [`hwɔrfɪdʒ] *n.* 碼頭使用費
5 work out to 合計為

6 lawnmower [`lɔn‚moə] *n.* 割草機
7 accommodate [ə`kɑmə‚det] *v.* 容納
8 fabric softener [`fæbrɪk‚sɔfənə] *n.* 衣物柔軟精
9 take delivery 收取遞送的物品

Part 4

合約
Contracts

107 談論合約：一般情況
Referring to a Contract: General Conditions

☐ The (current) contract is up for[1] renewal[2] on July 31.

（目前的）合約得在七月三十一日續約。

☐ As it stands,[3] the current contact is/isn't likely to be renewed.[4]

照現在的情況來看，目前的合約很可能／不太可能會續約。

☐ Yoyodyne is looking to renegotiate[5] their contract with the city.

優優戴恩想要和市府重新協商他們的合約。

☐ We have honored[6] both the letter[7] and the spirit of the contract.

我們已經履行了合約的條文和精神。

☐ The parties have (certain) obligations[8] under the contract (terms).

在合約（的規定）下，各方都有（某些）義務。

☐ Textrite has clearly repudiated[9] the terms of the contract by failing to make payment.

泰絲特萊很明顯地以未付款的方式拒絕接受合約的條件。

---

[1] up for 打算……；考慮要……
[2] renewal [rɪˋnuəl] *n.* （契約等的）重訂
[3] as it stands 照目前的情況看來
[4] renew [rɪˋnu] *v.* 更新；重訂（契約等的）期限
[5] renegotiate [ˌrinɪˋgoʃɪˏet] *v.* 再協商
[6] honor [ˋɑnɚ] *v.* 履行（協議等）
[7] letter [ˋlɛtɚ] *n.* 字面上的意義
[8] obligation [ˏɑbləˋgeʃən] *n.* 義務；責任
[9] repudiate [rɪˋpjudɪˏet] *v.* 拒絕接受

108 談論合約：特定條款
Referring to a Contract: Specific Clauses[1]

☐ The contract contains a(n) arbitration[2] clause.
合約包含一條仲裁條款。

☐ The contract (clearly) stipulates[3] that all sales are F.O.B.
合約（清楚地）訂明所有的銷售都是船上交貨價。

☐ Termination[4] without notice is precluded[5] by paragraph 17(a).
第 17(a) 項禁止未經事前通知即中止合約。

☐ The contract terms establish liability/responsibility for negligence.[6]
合約條件明訂對疏失應負有的義務／責任。

☐ I'd direct your attention to paragraph 14 of the contract, which states/sets out[7] the inspection requirements.
我想請你注意一下合約的第 14 項，當中陳述／陳列了檢驗的要求。

☐ Responsibilities for arranging insurance are set out in paragraph 11(f), which reads: "lessee[8] shall arrange for adequate insurance coverage[9] for the premises."[10]
安排保險的責任在第 11(f) 項中有列明，上面說道：「承租人須負責為所承租之地物安排充分的保險。」

---

1 clause [klɔz] *n.* 條款
2 arbitration [ˌɑrbəˋtreʃən] *n.* 仲裁
3 stipulate [ˋstɪpjəˌlet] *v.* 約定
4 termination [ˌtɝməˋneʃən] *n.* 終結
5 preclude [prɪˋklud] *v.* 阻止；排除
6 negligence [ˋnɛglɪdʒəns] *n.* 疏忽；疏失

7 set out 陳列
8 lessee [lɛsˋi] *n.* 承租人
9 coverage [ˋkʌvərɪdʒ] *n.* 保險範圍
10 premises [ˋprɛmɪsɪz] *n.* 【複數型】建築物及其周圍的土地

109 修訂合約
Revising[1] a Contract

下列說法都可用「We can」或「Can we」來開頭，取決於你想陳述，還是發問。

陳述

☐ We can strike out[2] paragraph 18(e).

我們可以把第 18(e) 項刪除。

☐ We can change the wording[3] of the contract/clause.

我們可以改變合約／條款的用辭。

☐ We can insert the word "unlimited" before "discretion."

我們可以在「自行裁決」前面插入「不受限」這個詞。

詢問

☐ Can we amend[4] paragraph 3(b) to read "shall" instead of "may"?

我們是否可以把第 3(b) 項的「得以」修改成「必須」？

☐ Can we add a new sub-paragraph to paragraph 24 to reflect the change?

我們是否可以在第 24 項中添加一條新的子項來反映這個改變？

☐ Can we have the legal department draft[5] a clause that sets out our respective[6] obligations when it comes to advertising?

我們可否讓法務部門草擬一項條款，明訂我們各自在作廣告時應有的義務？

---

1 revise [rɪ`vaɪz] v. 修正；修訂
2 strike out 刪除
3 wording [`wɜdɪŋ] n. 措辭

4 amend [ə`mɛnd] v. 修改
5 draft [dræft] v. 草擬；起草
6 respective [rɪ`spɛktɪv] adj. 個別的；各自的

110 簽訂合約
Signing a Contract

☐ I'll need your signature[1] here, please.

我需要請你在這裡簽名。

☐ The witnesses[2] will sign here and here.

見證人要在這裡和這裡簽名。

☐ Please initial[3] every page of the document.

請在文件的每一頁簽上姓名縮寫。

☐ We'll have to initial each amendment[4] we've made.

我們必須在我們做的每一項修訂上簽上姓名縮寫。

☐ If you'll be so good as to sign and date[5] the document, please.

麻煩你在文件上簽上姓名和日期。

☐ This is my name chop.[6] It has the same effect as a signature in my country.

這是我的印章。在我的國家它的效力等同於簽名。

---

1 signature [`sɪgnətʃə·] *n.* 簽名
2 witness [`wɪtnɪs] *n.* 目擊者；見證人
3 initial [ɪ`nɪʃəl] *v.* 簽姓名的首字母（於文件上）

4 amendment [ə`mɛndmənt] *n.* 改正；修正（案）
5 date [det] *v.* 寫上日期
6 name chop [`nem͵tʃɑp] *n.* 印章

Part 5

法律與政策議題
Legal and Policy Issues

引用法律與法令
Referring to Laws and Regulations

☐ The Tenancies Act[1] is the law applicable[2] to landlord[3]-tenant[4] disputes.
《租賃法》是適用於房東與住客間紛爭的法律。

☐ The law isn't clear on the issue of vicarious[5] liability in this situation.
法律對於在這種情況下責任轉承問題的規範並不清楚。

☐ The regulations for importing tropical fish are set out in the Live Animals Import Act.
進口熱帶魚的相關法令明訂在《活體動物進口法》中。

☐ The Fair Packaging and Labeling[6] Act limits on the claims you can legally make.
《公平包裝與標示法》裡明訂你們可以依法提出索賠要求的限制。

☐ Have a look at the regulations. Our respective rights/responsibilities are all clearly spelled out.[7]
看看這些法令。我們各自的權利／責任都明白地列出。

☐ By law, we're/you're required to report a change of address within thirty days.
我們／你們依法必須在三十天內通報地址變更。

---

1 Tenancies Act [ˈtɛnənsɪz ˌækt] n. 【法】租賃法案

2 applicable [ˈæplɪkəbl] adj. 適用的

3 landlord [ˈlænd.lɔrd] n. 地主；房東

4 tenant [ˈtɛnənt] n. 房客；佃農

5 vicarious [vaɪˈkɛrɪəs] adj. 代理的；代替的

6 labeling [ˈleblɪŋ] n. 標示

7 spell out 詳細說明

112

規避法律與法令
Getting Around[1] Laws and Regulations

MP3 114

☐ There's a loophole[2] that we can use to our advantage.
有一個漏洞我們可以利用。

☐ The Copyright Act may not apply to[3] us if we wait another two years.
如果我們再等個兩年，《著作權法》也許就不適用於我們了。

☐ It might be possible to avoid complying with[4] the mall regulations about signage.[5]
規避購物中心關於招牌的規定也許是可能的。

☐ We can skirt[6] the zoning[7] bylaws[8] by calling the bar a restaurant, and getting a restaurant license instead.
我們可以把酒吧改稱為餐廳，取得餐廳執照，這樣就可以規避區域規畫細則。

☐ We may be able to get around the quarantine[9] regulations by providing the proof of inoculation[10] documents beforehand.
我們也許可以事先提供接種疫苗的證明文件，以規避隔離規定。

☐ There's a chance we can put ourselves outside the reach/operation of the law by opening an office in Bermuda.
我們可以在百慕達設立一個分公司，這樣就有可能不受法律的規範／現行法律的約束。

Part 5 法律與政策議題

---

1 get around 規避；逃避
2 loophole [`lup͵hol] *n.* （法律等的）漏洞
3 apply to 應用於；施用於
4 comply with 遵從
5 signage [`saɪnɪdʒ] *n.* 【總稱】招牌

6 skirt [`skɝt] *v.* 避開（困難、問題等）
7 zoning [`zonɪŋ] *n.* 都市的區域劃分
8 bylaw [`baɪ͵lɔ] *n.* 地方法；細則
9 quarantine [`kwɔrən͵tin] *n.* 隔離；檢疫
10 inoculation [ɪn͵ɑkjə`leʃən] *n.* 預防接種

Section *4* 特定的談判議題 185

☐ We're amenable[3] to an out-of-court[4] settlement.
我們願意進行庭外和解。

☐ We'd like to settle (this) as much as you would.
我們和你們一樣想要（就這件事）和解。

☐ This settlement offer is made without prejudice.[5]
這項和解提議不帶任何偏見。

☐ The settlement package we propose contains/includes back[6] wages.
我們提議的和解方案中包含／包括了過去積欠的薪資。

☐ We're prepared to offer two hundred thousand dollars to compensate[7] you for damage to your firm's reputation.
我們準備提供二十萬元來補償你們公司的名譽損失。

☐ We're seeking compensation for our losses in the amount of two point two million euros[8] (€ 2,200,000).
針對我們的損失，我們要求總計兩百二十萬歐元的賠償。

---

1 settlement [ˈsɛtlmənt] *n.* 和解；解決
2 compensation [ˌkɑmpənˈseʃən] *n.* 賠償
3 amenable [əˈminəbl] *adj.* 願順從的
4 out-of-court [ˈaut əv ˈkɔrt] *adj.* 庭外的
5 prejudice [ˈprɛdʒədɪs] *n.* 偏見
6 back [bæk] *adj.* 積欠的；拖欠的
7 compensate [ˈkɑmpənˌset] *v.* 賠償
8 euro [ˈjuro] *n.* 歐元

114 法律權利與執照
Legal Rights and Licenses

☐ The scope[1] of the license is broad/narrow.

這張執照的範圍很廣／窄。

☐ The license is transferable/non-transferable.[2]

這張執照可轉讓／不可轉讓。

☐ RadioShack retains[3]/assumes[4] the right to perform the work publicly.

雷迪歐謝克保留／擁有公開表演這項作品的權利。

☐ The rights to modify[5] the program would remain with/transfer[6] to Mr. Green.

修改節目的權利由格林先生保有／轉讓給格林先生。

☐ The license would give Megatrend the right to reproduce, display, and sell the copyrighted materials.

這張執照將給予鉅潮重製、展示與銷售已取得版權之作品的權利。

☐ The licensor[7] grants[8] the licensee[9] the right to use the trademark[10] in their promotional materials.

授權人給予受權人於其促銷文宣中使用該商標的權利。

1 scope [skop] *n.* 範圍
2 (non-)transferable [(ˌnɑn) trænsˋfɝəbl] *adj.* （不）可移轉的；（不）可讓渡的
3 retain [rɪˋten] *v.* 保留；保有
4 assume [əˋsum] *v.* 承擔；採用；僭取；霸佔
5 modify [ˋmɑdəˌfaɪ] *v.* 修正

6 transfer [trænsˋfɝ] *v.* 轉移；讓渡（後接介系詞 to）
7 licensor [ˋlaɪsnsə] *n.* 授權者
8 grant [grænt] *v.* 允許；答應
9 licensee [ˌlaɪsnˋsi] *n.* 受權者
10 trademark [ˋtredˌmɑrk] *n.* 商標

Part 5 法律與政策議題

Section

5

策略

Tactics

NEGOTIATION

Part 1

處於劣勢的談判
Negotiating from a
Weak Position

拖延
Delaying

談判策略

在談判中可以策略性地運用時間來改變優勢的平衡點。有時候你討價還價的能力會隨著時間的過去、愈來愈接近期限而升高。在這樣的情況下，時間可能會造成對手的壓力。另外也可能會有些情況讓你想晚點再作出決定。下列這些說法反映出不同的拖延戰術。

☐ Let's wrap up[1] early today.

我們今天早點結束吧。

☐ I forgot to bring the affidavit[2] with me.

我忘了帶宣誓書來。

☐ We're not going to be able to make the meeting.

我們沒辦法趕上會議了。

☐ I am waiting for further instructions from the head office.[3]

我在等總公司的進一步指示。

☐ We're going to need some time to think/talk this over.

我們需要一些時間來思考／討論這件事。

---

1 wrap up 結束
2 affidavit [ˌæfəˈdevɪt] *n.* 宣誓書；口供書
3 head office [ˈhɛd ˌɔfɪs] *n.* 總公司

□ I'm still waiting on the translation of the documents.

我還在等文件的翻譯。

□ We'd feel much more comfortable if we could change the venue.[4]

如果我們可以換場地，我們會覺得自在許多。

□ We're going to have a personnel[5] change and it will take us a while to bring our new team member up to speed.[6]

我們即將會有人事變動，我們需要一些時間才能讓我們的新隊員進入狀況。

□ Dick Richards is feeling under the weather.[7] Would it be OK with you if we adjourned[8] early?

迪克・理查德身體不適。你們同不同意我們今天早點休會？

□ We can't possibly have our evaluation of the proposal ready by Friday. You've got to give us more time.

我們不可能在星期五前準備好我們對提案的評估。你們得給我們更多時間。

Part 1 處於劣勢的談判

---

[4] venue [ˋvɛnju] *n.* 集合場地；舉辦地點
[5] personnel [͵pɝsṇˋɛl] *adj.* 人事的；人員的
[6] bring sb. up to speed 使某人進入狀況
[7] under the weather 【口語】身體不適
[8] adjourn [əˋdʒɝn] *v.* 休會

116 增加多方參與者與建立同盟關係
Increasing the Number of Parties and Coalition[1] Building

談判策略

數大就是力量。與其他人結盟以利用他們的能力、構想與資源，通常都會對你有利。有時候你可能想與坐在談判桌對面的人建立關係；有時候你可能想引進第三方來參與討論。不管是哪一種情況，你都需要下列的說法來說服別人。

☐ It's imperative that we present a united front.[2]

我們必須站在同一陣線。

☐ We should be seeking to ally[3] ourselves with Alcosell.

我們應該尋求和艾可賽結盟。

☐ It's in our/everyone's best interest to work together on this.

在這件事上合作對我們／大家最有利。

☐ If we don't all stick together, there's no way this is going to work.

如果我們不團結在一起，這是不可能行得通的。

☐ What would you say if I suggested we bring in[4] a consultant?[5]

如果我建議我們邀請一位顧問參加，你覺得如何？

---

1 coalition [ˌkoəˋlɪʃən] *n.* 聯盟；結合
2 front [frʌnt] *n.* 戰線；陣線（present a united front 指站在同一陣線）
3 ally [əˋlaɪ] *v.* 締結同盟
4 bring in 邀請（顧問、協助者）參加
5 consultant [kənˋsʌltənt] *n.* 顧問

☐ Things will move a lot quicker if we invite a delegation[6] from Honeywell to join us at the table.

如果我們邀請漢尼威爾的代表團加入我們的會談，事情會進行得快許多。

☐ We would all really benefit from the expertise[7] of (somebody like) Kelsey Robinson.

我們都會大大受益於（像）凱西‧羅賓森（這樣的人）的專業知識。

☐ We all stand to gain by forming a strategic alliance[8] with Hollings.

和霍林斯締結策略聯盟，對我們都可能有好處。

☐ If we invite someone from the arbitration board, we're bound to[9] make better progress.

如果我們邀請某位仲裁委員加入，我們一定會有更好的進展。

☐ We should consider working in partnership with the Society for Promotion of the Visual Arts.

我們應該考慮和視覺藝術促進協會合作。

Part I 處於劣勢的談判

---

6 delegation [ˌdɛdʒləˋgeʃən] *n.* 代表團
7 expertise [ˌɛkspɚˋtiz] *n.* 專門技術；專業技術
8 strategic alliance [strəˋtidʒɪk ˌəˋlaɪəns] *n.* 策略同盟
9 be bound to 一定會

117 既成事實
Fait Accompli[1]

談判策略

有時候你可能會處於一種狀況:事已成定局,而你必須告知對方。相反地,也可能是你的對手處於這種狀況。不論是前者還是後者,已成定局的事實有可能會限制某一方的選擇。

☐ It's too late for that.

要那麼做已經太遲了。

☐ Sorry. It's already a done[2] deal.

抱歉,這件事已成定局。

☐ You missed the boat,[3] I'm afraid.

恐怕你錯過機會了。

☐ We can't undo[4] what's already been done.

我們無法挽回既成的事實。

☐ It's already been settled/decided/approved.

這事已經解決/決定了/批准了。

---

1 fait accompli [fɛtakõˋpli] *n.* 【法文】既成事實

2 done [dʌn] *adj.* 完成的

3 miss the boat 錯過機會

4 undo [ˌʌnˋdu] *v.* 使……還原

☐ That matter was put to rest[5]/decided a long time ago.

那件事很久以前就已經定案／決定了。

☐ We're expecting an (official) announcement[6] on the merger any time now.

我們現在隨時都在等待合併案的（正式）公布。

☐ You're too late. It's already been done/gone through/approved.

你太遲了。這事已經完成／通過／批准了。

☐ It shouldn't come as a surprise to you that we've already contacted Micro-Sun Unlimited to verify[7] your claims.

你們不應該驚訝我們已經與微陽無限公司聯絡，以印證你們的說法。

☐ As you might have expected, we've already accepted the bid from Talesco for the Kaohsiung project.

正如你們可能預期的，我們已經接受了泰斯可對高雄專案的出價。

---

5 put to rest 已經定案的
6 announcement [ə`naʊnsmənt] *n.* 宣布
7 verify [`vɛrə,faɪ] *v.* 證實

118 承諾
Promising

談判策略

一諾值千金,所以承諾不要輕易說出口。如果你答應要做某件事,就應該盡全力來完成。畢竟,名聲要用一輩子的時間來建立,但卻可能毀於一旦。

☐ I give you my word. / You have my word.

我向你保證。／你有我的保證。

☐ I swear on my life I will never miss a payment again.

我以性命擔保絕不會再漏付款項。

☐ I vow to clean up[1] my act and right[2] the wrongs[3] I have done.

我發誓會處理好我的所做所為並補救我所犯的過錯。

☐ I promise you this will be the last you hear from us about the matter.

我跟你保證,這會是你最後一次聽我們提這件事。

☐ I can guarantee you a minimum order from us of twenty-five thousand units.

我可以向你保證,我們最少會下兩萬五千個的訂單。

---

1 clean up 收拾;處理
2 right [raɪt] v. 糾正;改正
3 wrong [rɔŋ] n. 不當的行為

☐ You have my personal promise to send that cheque[4] out to you first thing in the morning.[5]

我個人向你保證，明天一大早就會把那張支票寄給你。

☐ I'll go on record as saying there will be no fare[6] increase this year.

我會公開地說今年票價不會調漲。

☐ I can unequivocally[7] state that I am committed one-hundred percent to this endeavor.[8]

我可以明確地說，我承諾會付出百分之百的努力來做這件事。

☐ I'll do whatever it takes to get to the bottom of[9] this.

我會盡一切努力來查明這件事的真相。

☐ You have a firm commitment from us to refrain[10] from using your image in our magazine in the future.

您有我們堅定的承諾，我們未來不會在我們的雜誌裡使用您的肖像。

Part
1

處
於
劣
勢
的
談
判

---

4 cheque [tʃɛk] *n.* 【英】支票（=【美】check）

5 first thing in the morning 明天早上第一件事（指明天一大早就優先處理）

6 fare [fɛr] *n.* 車費；（飛機等的）票價

7 unequivocally [ˌʌnɪˋkwɪvəklɪ] *adv.* 明確

地；不含糊地

8 endeavor [ɪnˋdɛvɚ] *n.* 努力（做的任務、事業等）

9 get to the bottom of 查明⋯⋯的真相

10 refrain [rɪˋfren] *v.* 克制（後接介系詞 from）

連結
Linking

談判策略

將議題連結在一起可以開啓新的契機，也可以提供某一方談判的施力點，特別是當「package deal」（整套交易）比一項項個別議題分開來解決更有利時。在談判的語言中，「連結」可以同時意謂著穩固你的立場和玩禮尚往來的遊戲。

☐ Job security is part and parcel[1] of a collective agreement.[2]
工作的穩定性是共同協議中的重要部分。

☐ I'm not willing to separate those issues. It's all or nothing here.
我不願意將這些議題分開。要不就是全部，要不就都免談。

☐ The production quota[3] can't be looked at/considered in isolation.[4]
生產配額不能單獨來看／考慮。

☐ This decision should be seen as part of a larger market entry strategy.
這項決策應該被視為進入市場較大策略的一部分。

☐ The trespassing[5] issue can't be settled independently of the noise bylaw issue.
非法入侵的議題不能不考慮噪音細則的議題而單獨解決。

---

[1] part and parcel 重要部分；主要部分
[2] collective agreement [kəˈlɛktɪv əˈɡrimənt] n. 共同協議
[3] quota [ˈkwotə] n. 定額；配額
[4] in isolation 單獨地
[5] trespass [ˈtrɛspəs] v. 侵入他人土地、住宅等

☐ The issue of product liability goes hand in hand[6] with the issue of outsourcing[7] production.
產品責任的議題和外包生產的議題息息相關。

☐ If you agree to our shipping terms, then I'll guarantee a price below twenty-two fifty ($22.50).
如果你同意我們的運送條件，我就可以允諾低於二十二元五十分的價格。

☐ As you're willing to provide your own transportation, I'm willing to waive[8] our storage fees in exchange.
因為你們願意提供自己的運輸工具，我願意免除我們的倉儲費用作為交換。

☐ Since we've agreed to print a retraction,[9] we think it's only fair to ask you to cancel the press conference.[10]
既然我們已經同意刊登收回說過的話，我們認為要求你們取消記者會應該很公平。

☐ To make things fair, we're offering to discount the order by ten percent (10%) to compensate you for your inconvenience.
為了公平起見，我們提議將訂單打一成的折扣，以補償你們的不便。

6 go hand in hand 息息相關
7 outsourcing [`aut͵sɔrsɪŋ] n. 外包
8 waive [wev] v. 宣佈放棄
9 retraction [rɪ`trækʃən] n. 取消；撤回
10 press conference [`prɛs͵kɑnfərəns] n. 記者會

120 個人化
Personalizing[1]

(!) 談判策略

讓事情變得個人化可以讓你轉而訴諸人性的情感。道德訴求通常有效，不過前提是你的道德必須無懈可擊。提及你對於對方的歷史、家庭狀況、經濟狀況等所知的內幕消息也一樣有效。

☐ Don't let your teamates[2] down.

不要讓你的組員失望。

☐ You know it's the right thing to do.

你知道這是應該做的事。

☐ Make the right decision, Mr. Mitsumoto.

做出正確的決定，光本先生。

☐ We both know where your real interests lie.

我們都知道你們真正的利益何在。

☐ You're not exactly in a position to issue[3] ultimatums.[4]

你並不真的有立場下最後通牒。

---

1 personalize [ˋpɝsn̩ˌaɪz] v. 個人化；針對個人

2 teammate [ˋtimˌmet] n. 隊友；組員

3 issue [ˋɪʃu] v. 發出（命令、布告等）

4 ultimatum [ˌʌltəˋmetəm] n. 最後通牒

☐ Think of your father, Steven. What would he do in your position?
想想你的父親，史蒂芬。如果他在你的立場，會怎麼做？

☐ I thought I could count on[5] you to get our sales team back on track.[6]
我以為我可以指望你讓我們的銷售團隊重新步上軌道。

☐ Have you stopped to think about what this means/would mean for your family?
你有沒有停下來想一想，這對你的家人而言意味／會意味什麼？

☐ I know your brother would have wanted you to see this project through to completion.[7]
我知道你的哥哥一定會想要你有始有終地完成這項計畫。

☐ I should think that a person in your circumstances[8]/situation would leap at[9] an opportunity like this.
我會認為處於你這種情況／情形的人會迫不及待地抓住這樣的機會。

---

5 count on 依靠；指望
6 on track 上軌道；不離題
7 see sth. through to completion 有始有終地完成某事
8 circumstance [ˈsɜkəm.stæns] *n.* 情況（常用複數）
9 leap at sth. 迫不及待地爭取某事物

Part 2

處於優勢的談判
Negotiating from a Position
of Power

121 提及你的其他選擇
Mentioning Your Other Options

MP3 123

談判策略

有時候，提醒對方你尚有其他選擇是一種有效的談判手法。不過要小心，這種策略有時會被解讀為傲慢而產生負作用，造成你不樂見的效果，反而將對手推得更遠，並使你們的談判氣氛急轉直下、陷入僵局。

☐ We don't need this deal. We have other options.
我們不需要這筆交易。我們有其他的選擇。

☐ You should know, we're entertaining[1] other offers.
你們應該要知道，我們還在考慮其他的提議。

☐ We've also received an offer from one of your competitors.
我們也收到了你們一名競爭對手的提議。

☐ Your application/proposal/bid is one of several being considered.
你們的申請／提案／出價是我們列入考慮的其中之一。

☐ If this doesn't pan out,[2] we can always go back to using our suppliers in Vietnam.
如果這件事不成功，我們總還是可以回頭找我們在越南的供應商。

---

1 entertain [ˌɛntəˈten] v. 採納；考慮（意見、看法等）
2 pan out 【口語】成功；有成果（常用於否定句或疑問句）

談判 900 句典

□ One way or another,[3] the success or failure of these negotiations won't make us or break us.[4]

不論如何，這些談判的成或敗並不會造就我們或摧毀我們。

□ If this doesn't go through,[5] we'll be quite content[6] to carry on doing business exactly as before.

如果這件事不能順利完成，我們會相當滿足於像以前那樣繼續作生意。

□ Several of your competitors have also expressed an interest in entering into[7] a distribution deal.

你們的幾個競爭對手對參與經銷也表示了興趣。

□ Our fallback[8] option is to sign a three-year lease for the Bank Street location with Levinson Property Company.

我們的備案就是和賴文森房地產公司簽訂一張班克街那個地點的三年租約。

□ If you don't want to do business, we can always contact another supplier/manufacturer/retailer/financial institution.

如果你們不想作生意，我們總還是能和另一家供應商／製造商／零售商／金融機構聯繫。

---

3 one way or another 反正；無論如何
4 make sb. or break sb. 造就某人或摧毀某人
5 go through 順利完成
6 content [kənˋtɛnt] *adj.* 滿足於
7 enter into 投身於……；成為……的一部分
8 fallback [ˋfɔl͵bæk] *n.* 撤退；備案

要求做決定
Demanding a Decision

談判策略

如果王牌全握在你手上，你便有較佳的優勢和立場；你可以根據你的時程表來要求對方作出決定。這種方法通常會讓對方倍感壓力。

☐ Yes, or no?

好還是不好？

☐ It's your move.

該你採取行動了。

☐ What's your call?[1]

你的決定是什麼？

☐ What have you decided?

你做了什麼決定？

☐ So, what's it going to be?

那，答案是什麼？

---

1 call [kɔl] *n.* 決定

☐ We need to know your decision/answer.

我們需要知道你們的決定／回答。

☐ We've been patient and given you all the time in the world.[2]

我們一直很有耐心，也給了你們充分的時間。

☐ We need a decision now/by the end of the day/by next week.

我們現在／今天結束之前／下週之前就需要一個決定。

☐ It's your call. But we need to know by tomorrow/Tuesday/
January 1.

由你決定。但是我們需要在明天／星期二／一月一日前知道。

☐ You've had ample[3] time to consider your options. What's your
answer?

你已經有充分的時間考慮你的選擇了。你的答案是什麼？

---

[2] all the time in the world 非常充裕的時間
[3] ample [ˋæmpl] *adj.* 足夠的；充分的

123 威脅退出
Threatening to Walk Away

談判策略

如果對方拒絕作出關鍵的讓步、表現得蠻不講理，或是使用你不認同的策略，你可以威脅要退出談判。當然，這可以用來唬人。但是當你在虛張聲勢時，千萬要小心，因為你的對手可能會說：「Fine. Go ahead.」。退出談判真的對你最有利嗎？應該要先想清楚你的底限是什麼。

☐ I'm not afraid to walk.

我可不怕走人。

☐ If you think I'm bluffing,[1] test me.

如果你覺得我是在唬人，那就試試。

☐ I think we've said everything there is to say.

我覺得我們該說的都說了。

☐ If you keep making threats, I'm out the door.

如果你繼續威脅恐嚇，我就走人。

☐ This is turning out to be a waste of my/both our time.

這變成是在浪費我的／我們雙方的時間。

---

1 bluff [blʌf] *v.* 虛張聲勢以騙人；嚇唬人

☐ I see no point in dragging this out[2] (unnecessarily). I thank you for your time.

我看不出繼續（不必要地）拖下去有什麼意義。謝謝你的時間。

☐ Why should I stay here if you're going to keep me in the dark[3] about the merger plans?

如果你打算瞞著我合併計畫的事，我為何還要留在這兒？

☐ I don't think there's much chance of us coming to an agreement. Perhaps I should go ....

我認為我們達成協議的機會不大。也許我該離開……

☐ I'm out of here unless you pick up the phone and call Mike Lawson and speak to him yourself.

除非你拿起電話打給邁克‧勞森並親自和他談，否則我就走人。

☐ If you won't make some concession[4] on wage demands, we don't have anything more to say to one another.

如果你不肯在薪資要求上作一些讓步，我們彼此就沒什麼好說的了。

---

[2] drag out 拖延
[3] keep sb. in the dark 把某人蒙在鼓裏
[4] make concession [kən`sɛʃən] 讓步

威脅採取法律行動
Threatening Legal Action

談判策略

如果你知道你在法律上站得住腳，你可以使用法律訴訟的威脅來作為談判手段。沒有人會想要走上法律一途，即使是律師本身亦然。

☐ I'll see you in court.

我和你法庭見。

☐ You'll be hearing from my lawyer.

我的律師會跟你聯絡。

☐ There are several legal remedies[1] we can pursue.[2]

我們可以尋求幾個法律上的彌補措施。

☐ We'll be filing suit[3]/an appeal[4] in the District Court.[5]

我們會在地方法院提出訴訟／上訴。

☐ Do that, and you can expect a counter suit[6] from us.

那麼做的話，你們就等著我們提出抗告吧。

---

1 remedy [ˋrɛmədɪ] *n.* 補救方法
2 pursue [pəˋsu] *v.* 尋求；遵從
3 file (a) suit 控告；提出訴訟
4 file an appeal [əˋpil] 提出上訴
5 District Court [ˋdɪstrɪktˏkort] *n.* 地方法院
6 counter suit [ˋkauntəˏsut] *n.* 抗告

☐ We'll ask the courts to settle the matter once and for all.

我們會要求法院一勞永逸地解決這件事。

☐ We'll apply to the courts to grant[7] a temporary[8] injunction.[9]

我們會向法院申請核發臨時禁制令。

☐ We'll be seeking compensation for the cost of the repairs to our vehicle.

我們會尋求賠償修理車子的花費。

☐ We'll sue[10] for lost wages, damage to reputation, and emotional anguish.[11]

我們會針對薪資損失、名譽受損和精神傷害提出告訴。

☐ If you don't cease[12] and desist[13] immediately, we'll be forced to take legal action.

如果你們不馬上停止並打消這個念頭，我們將被迫採取法律行動。

---

7 grant [ˋɡrænt] *v.* （答應請求而正式地）給予
8 temporary [ˋtɛmpəˏrɛrɪ] *adj.* 臨時的
9 injunction [ɪnˋdʒʌŋkʃən] *n.* 禁止令
10 sue [su] *v.* 控告

11 anguish [ˋæŋgwɪʃ] *n.* （身心上的）極度痛苦
12 cease [sis] *v.* 中止；停止
13 desist [dɪˋzɪst] *v.* 停止；斷念；對……死心

最後通牒
Ultimatums

談判策略

當你大權在握時，拿「要不要隨你」的標準台詞來威嚇對方，通常是件容易的事。但是當然，請確定你有準備好備用計畫，以免他們決定「不要」。還有，如果你討價還價的立場比對方薄弱，你或許可以用下列幾個最後通牒的方式來虛張聲勢。

☐ Are you in or out?[1]

你是要加入還是退出？

☐ That's our final offer.

那是我們最後的提議。

☐ Do you agree, or not?

你是同意，還是不同意？

☐ That's not a threat; it's a promise.

那不是威脅，那是承諾。

☐ That's our offer; take it or leave it.[2]

那是我們的提議，要不要隨你們。

---

[1] in or out　加入或退出
[2] take it or leave it　要不要隨你

☐ You're leaving us no alternative[3] but to go public[4] with the information.

你們讓我們別無選擇，只能將這個資訊公開。

☐ We're giving you a choice: accept our list of demands or get ready for a strike.[5]

我們給你們一個選擇：接受我們列出的要求，不然就準備面對罷工。

☐ If you continue to delay shipment, we'll have no choice but to cancel the order.

如果你們繼續延遲出貨，我們就別無選擇，只好取消訂單。

☐ Should you refuse our offer, our only recourse[6] would be to go ahead with the eviction.[7]

如果你拒絕我們的提議，我們唯一的途徑就是進行驅逐。

☐ If you insist on violating[8] the terms of the contract, we won't hesitate[9] to terminate[10] this relationship.

如果你堅持要違反合約的條件，我們會毫不猶豫地中止這個關係。

---

3 alternative [ɔl`tɜnətɪv] *n.* 其他可採取的方法、選擇
4 go public 公開
5 strike [straɪk] *n.* 罷工
6 recourse [rɪ`kors] *n.* 求助；依靠
7 eviction [ɪ`vɪkʃən] *n.* 逐出；驅逐
8 violate [`vaɪə͵let] *v.* 違反
9 hesitate [`hɛzə͵tet] *v.* 猶豫
10 terminate [`tɜmə͵net] *v.* 終止；結束

126 突顯你的優勢
Asserting[1] Your Strengths[2]

談判策略

談判就是推銷，推銷的可能是你自己、你的觀點、你的提議、你的公司或是你的產品。「自賣自誇」讓別人知道你的長處並不是虛榮，而是說服對方讓對方聽你說話的方式之一。好好利用這個策略。

☐ Our customer service is second to none.[3]

我們的顧客服務不亞於任何人。

☐ We have considerable[4] expertise in web page design.

我們在網頁設計上有相當豐富的專業。

☐ Our/My reputation (in the ad industry) speaks for itself.[5]

我們／我（在廣告界）的名聲不說自明。

☐ We've built our reputation on honesty and straightforwardness.[6]

我們的名聲建立在誠信與坦率上。

☐ I have over twenty years experience in the public relations business.

我在公關業有超過二十年的經驗。

---

1 assert [ə`sɝt] *v.* 力陳；聲明；斷言
2 strength [strɛŋθ] *n.* 長處；優勢
3 second to none 【口語】不亞於任何人
4 considerable [kən`sɪdərəbl] *adj.* 相當多的

5 speak for itself 不說自明
6 straightforwardness [͵stret`fɔrwɚdnɪs] *n.* 坦率；直率

☐ We didn't get to where we are today by backing down[7] from fights.

我們會有今天的地位，可不是因為我們會不戰而降。

☐ Our place in the market speaks volumes[8] about our commitment to innovation.

我們在市場中的地位充分地證明了我們對於創新的投入。

☐ Our strength lies in the fact that we use locally produced raw materials.[9]

我們的優勢在於一個事實，那就是我們使用當地生產的原物料。

☐ Our market share[10] reflects[11] the quality of the workmanship that goes into our products.

我們的市場占有率反映出我們產品製造的手工品質。

☐ Our longevity[12] (in the industry) is a testament[13] to the satisfaction of our customers.

我們（在業界）的悠久歷史是顧客滿意的證明。

Part 2 處於優勢的談判

---

[7] back down 放棄；讓步
[8] speak volumes 充分地證明
[9] raw material [ˋrɔ məˋtɪrɪəl] n. 原料
[10] market share [ˋmɑrkɪt.ʃɛr] n. 市場占有率
[11] reflect [rɪˋflɛkt] v. 反映
[12] longevity [lɑnˋdʒɛvətɪ] n. 長命；長壽
[13] testament [ˋtɛstəmənt] n. 證明

恭維

Flattery[1]

MP3 129

談判策略

小小的恭維可能會有大大的效果。在適當的時機給予適當的恭維，可以讓對方感覺得到自己的價值，並進而將這種感覺轉化為對談判的自在與滿意。這些正面的感受可能會讓對方更加願意同意你的要求。

☐ You're a credit[2] to your profession.[3]
你是你那一行的榮耀。

☐ Well put. I couldn't have said it better myself.
說得好。我自己肯定沒辦法說得更好。

☐ What you said makes complete/eminent[4] sense.
你說的完全／非常有道理。

☐ Of course we recognize everything you've done for the company.
當然我們體認你為公司所做的每件事。

☐ I don't doubt for a moment you have every intention of making good on[5] the terms of the contract.
我從不懷疑你非常有心要履行合約的條件。

1. flattery [`flætərɪ] *n.* 奉承
2. credit [`krɛdɪt] *n.* 帶來榮耀的人
3. profession [prə`fɛʃən] *n.* 職業；專業
4. eminent [`ɛmənənt] *adj.* 卓越的；傑出的
5. make good on (sth.) 實現、實踐（某事）
6. stature [`stætʃɚ] *n.* 地位；高度；聲譽；水平
7. one's hat is off to 某人向……致敬
8. turn around 扭轉局面；扭轉劣勢

☐ It's an honor for us to have the chance to meet with someone of your stature.[6]

有機會和您這樣有地位的人見面是我們的榮幸。

☐ Our hats are off to[7] you for taking the initiative and turning your company around.[8]

我們要向你致敬，因為你率先行動扭轉你們公司的劣勢。

☐ We're grateful for your hard work / efforts in building this coalition.

我們很感謝你為了建立聯盟所付出的辛勞／努力。

☐ Someone with your intelligence / business savvy[9] / convictions[10] must surely hate to see opportunities fall by the wayside.[11]

像你這樣有聰明才智／業界知識／信念的人，一定很痛恨看到機會白白錯失。

☐ I would never for a single moment question your perseverance[12] / dedication / commitment.

我永遠都不會質疑你的毅力／奉獻／盡忠職守。

☐ You have a well-earned[13] reputation for being honest / straight-forward / resourceful.[14]

你誠信／坦率／機智的名聲是你應得的。

---

9 savvy [`sævɪ] *n.* 見識；理解能力

10 conviction [kən`vɪkʃən] *n.* 信念

11 fall by the wayside 棄置；半途而廢

12 perseverance [ˌpɜsə`vɪrəns] *n.* 堅忍不拔；堅持不懈

13 well-earned [`wɛl.ɜnd] *adj.* 憑自己力量得來的；正當獲得的

14 resourceful [rɪ`sorsfəl] *adj.* 富才智的；有應變才能的

Section

6

結果

Outcomes

陷入僵局
At an Impasse[1]

☐ This isn't going to work out.

這不會成功的。

☐ We're at the end of our rope.[2]

我們已經無計可施了。

☐ We seem to have run out of options.

我們似乎已經沒有選擇了。

☐ I don't see any way to break this stalemate.[3]

我看不出有任何打破僵局的方法。

☐ It doesn't look like we're going to work this out.[4]

看來我們是沒辦法解決這件事了。

☐ We're obviously at an impasse, and I don't see any way around it.

我們很明顯陷入了僵局,而我看不出任何解決的方法。

---

1 impasse [ɪm`pæs] n. 僵局;絕境
2 at the end of one's rope 無計可施;智窮才盡
3 stalemate [`stel.met] n. 僵持狀態
4 work sth. out 解決某事

129 表達遺憾
Expressing Regret

☐ I hate to see jobs lost as much as you do, but we have to downsize.
我跟你一樣很不想看到有人失去工作，但是我們必須裁員。

☐ I wish it didn't have to be this way, but I guess I'll see you in court.
我希望事情不需要演變至此，但是我想咱們就法庭見吧。

☐ It pains[1] me to do it, but I'm going to have to make a formal complaint.
這麼做讓我很痛苦，但是我必須提出正式的申訴。

☐ It's a shame[2] to let an opportunity like this pass us by, but we can't agree to your terms.
錯失這樣的機會實在很可惜，但是我們無法同意你們的條件。

☐ It's regrettable,[3] but we have no choice but to press ahead[4] with the disciplinary[5] proceedings.[6]
真是令人遺憾，但是我們別無選擇，只能加緊進行紀律訴訟的程序。

☐ It's not an easy choice to make, but we're going to have to award[7] the contract to Pennyworth instead.
這不是一個容易的抉擇，但是我們必須改將合約給潘尼沃斯。

---

1 pain [pen] v. 使痛心
2 shame [ʃem] n. 令人惋惜的事
3 regrettable [rɪˋgrɛtəbl] adj. 令人遺憾的
4 press ahead 加緊進行（與介系詞 with 連用）
5 disciplinary [ˋdɪsəplɪn͵ɛrɪ] adj. 紀律的
6 proceedings [prəˋsidɪŋz] n.【法律】訴訟程序
7 award [əˋwɔrd] v.（經過慎重考慮後）給予

130 談判未果，離開時說的話
Things to Say Over Your Shoulder

如果談判沒有結果，下面是一些你離開時可以說的話。

☐ Call me if you change your mind.
如果你改變主意，打電話給我。

☐ Take some time to think about it.
花點時間想一下這件事。

☐ You should've taken us up on our offer.[1]
你們應該接受我們的提議的。

☐ If anything changes, you know where to reach me.
如果事情有任何改變，你知道要怎麼聯絡我。

☐ I'd urge[2] you to think it over[3] / reconsider. My door is always open.
我強烈地建議你認真考慮一下／重新考慮。我的大門永遠是敞開的。

☐ I have a feeling you're going to regret[4] this. Don't say I didn't warn you.
我有感覺你會後悔。別說我沒警告你。

---

1 take sb. up on sb.'s offer 接受某人的提議   **3** think sth. over 認真考慮某事
2 urge [ɜdʒ] v. 強烈建議；極力主張   **4** regret [rɪˋgrɛt] v. 懊悔；惋惜

131 不傷感情
No Hard Feelings

Section 6 結果

記住：對事不對人。如果無法達成協議，可以使用下列這些有風度的說法。

☐ We gave it our best shot.
我們盡了最大的努力。

☐ No one can say we didn't try.
沒有人能說我們沒有嘗試過。

☐ It's all water under the bridge.[1]
事情已經過去了。

☐ Some things just aren't meant to be.[2]
有些事情就是註定無法成真。

☐ It's unfortunate, but that's the way things go sometimes.
真是不幸，但是有時候事情就是如此。

☐ I was really looking forward to[3] collaborating[4] with you on this project.
我原本非常期待能夠和你合作這個專案。

---

[1] water under the bridge　過去的事；過眼雲煙

[2] meant to be　註定的

[3] look forward to (sth.)　期待（某事）

[4] collaborate [kə`læbə,ret] v. 合作

132 保持正面態度
Putting a Positive Spin[1] on Things

MP3 134

這些句子都可以在後面加上以「At least, ...」開頭的句子。

☐ It's not so bad.

事情沒有那麼糟。

☐ Look on the bright side.[2] At least some good came out of it.

往好的方面看，至少這事還是有一些好的結果。

☐ Things could be worse.

事情原本有可能更糟。

☐ The meeting wasn't / negotiations weren't a total loss.

這場會議／這幾回談判不完全是個失敗。

☐ Some good things came out of the meeting / negotiations.

這場會議／這幾回談判還是有一些好的結果。

☐ It looks bad now, but things will look better / improve in time.[3]

現在看起來很糟，但是過一段時間情況會看起來比較好／改善。

---

1 spin [spɪn] *n.* （獨特的）觀點；詮釋
2 look on the bright side　往好的方面看
3 in time　遲早；過一段時間

133 重述協議要點
Reiterating Points of Agreement

☐ OK. We see eye to eye[1] on the staffing[2] issue.

好，我們在人員配置的議題上同意彼此的看法。

☐ We're in agreement about the cover design issue.

我們在封面設計的議題上意見一致。

☐ At least we agree on the location for the conference.

至少我們在會議地點上達成了協議。

☐ Fortunately, we've reached a consensus[3] on lifting[4] the suspension.[5]

幸好我們在解除中止令上已經達成了共識。

☐ We're on the same page[6] when it comes to the importance of the customer loyalty program.[7]

在顧客忠誠度方案的重要性上，我們意見一致。

☐ We both recognize/acknowledge[8] the need to streamline[9] the production process.

我們雙方都體認到／承認需要簡化生產過程讓它更有效率。

---

1 see eye to eye 意見一致
2 staff [stæf] v. 提供人員配置
3 consensus [kən`sɛnsəs] n. 意見一致
4 lift [lɪft] v. 解除
5 suspension [sə`spɛnʃən] n. 中止；中斷

6 on the same page 意見一致
7 program [`prog ræm] n. 計劃；方案；綱領
8 acknowledge [ək`nɑlɪdʒ] v. 承認
9 streamline [`strim͵laɪn] v. 簡化使有效率

134 問題解決
Problem Solved

MP3 136

☐ That's settled.

那件事解決了。

☐ I'm glad we worked/sorted that out.[1]

我很高興我們把那件事解決／處理掉了。

☐ Adding a third shift solves the problem nicely.

增加第三個輪班順利地解決了問題。

☐ It's good to (finally) have that out of the way.[2]

（終於）把那件事解決了真好。

☐ The problem of holiday staffing seems to have solved itself.

假日人員配置的問題似乎自然地解決了。

☐ Settling the compensation issue opens the door to[3] rebuilding[4] the damaged relationship.

解決賠償的議題開啓了重建受損關係的契機。

---

1 sort out 處理；解決；澄清（問題、糾紛等）
2 have sth. out of the way 把某事解決掉
3 open the door to 對⋯⋯開放門戶；創造⋯⋯的機會；給與⋯⋯方便

4 rebuild [rɪ`bɪld] v. 改建；重建

135 討論未來的機會
Discussing Future Opportunities

和對方談判協議時，如果你用對方法，未來便有繼續合作的可能。

☐ Who knows where this could lead?

誰知道這將會有什麼後續發展？

☐ This represents just the tip[1] of the iceberg.[2]

這只代表著冰山的一角。

☐ This opens the door to a new era of mutual cooperation.

這開啟了一個雙方合作新紀元的契機。

☐ Although we won't make any money on the deal, it will pave the way[3] for more profitable agreements in the future.

雖然我們無法在這筆交易上賺到錢，但這會替未來更有獲利空間的協議鋪路。

☐ I see more collaborative[4] projects like this one in the future.

我預見未來會有更多類似這樣的合作計畫。

☐ The road ahead of us is full of opportunities to pool[5] our knowledge and reap[6] the profits.

我們眼前的路途充滿了可以匯集我們的知識並獲取利益的機會。

---

1 tip [tɪp] *n.* 尖端
2 iceberg [`aɪs‚bɝg] *n.* 冰山
3 pave the way 鋪路
4 collaborative [kə`læbəretɪv] *adj.* 合作的
5 pool [pul] *v.* 匯集
6 reap [rip] *v.* 收割；獲得

136 下一步
The Next Step

MP3 138

☐ **The next step is to** arrange to meet with the union reps.[1]
下一步就是要安排與工會代表碰面。

☐ **For now, the overriding[2] priority is** selling enough tickets.
就目前來說，最重要的優先事項就是要賣出足夠的票。

☐ **It's imperative that** we bring the other coalition members over to our side[3] ASAP.[4]
我們一定要盡快拉攏其他的同盟成員跟我們站在一邊。

☐ **Now that[5]** we've reached an agreement, **it behooves[6] us to** schedule a press conference.
既然我們已經達成了協議，我們理當安排一場記者會。

☐ **To make sure things keep moving along, I'll** have my assistant send you the paperwork first thing tomorrow morning.
為了確保事情繼續進行，我明兒一早就讓我的助理把文件送過去給你。

☐ **The task at hand is to** find a new supplier.
目前即將得做的工作就是要找到新的供應商。

---

1 rep [rɛp] *n.* 代表（representative 的簡稱）
2 overriding [ˋovəˏraɪdɪŋ] *adj.* 最重要的
3 bring sb. over to sb's side 拉攏某人使與某人同一陣線

4 ASAP 盡可能快（= as soon as possible）
5 now that 既然
6 behoove [bɪˋhuv] *v.* 使（人）責無旁貸；對（人）成爲義務

慶祝
Let's Celebrate!

☐ We've got a lot to celebrate!

我們有很多要慶祝的！

☐ This is an important day for all/both of us.

這對我們所有人／雙方都是重要的一天。

☐ We need to mark this momentous[1] occasion in fitting[2] style!

我們得用適當的方式來紀念這個意義非凡的時刻！

☐ Let's go get a drink./Let's adjourn[3] to the balcony[4] for a toast.[5]

我們去喝一杯吧。／我們休會到陽台上乾一杯吧。

☐ We'd like to invite you to join us for a celebratory[6] dinner.

我們想邀請你們跟我們一起去吃慶功晚宴。

☐ Ladies and Gentlemen, a toast to our new partnership!

各位先生、女士，為我們的新合夥關係乾杯！

---

1 momentous [moˋmɛntəs] *adj.* 重大的；
重要的
2 fitting [ˋfɪtɪŋ] *adj.* 適當的
3 adjourn [əˋdʒɝn] *v.* 休會；暫停（會議、審訊等）

4 balcony [ˋbælkənɪ] *n.* 陽台
5 toast [tost] *n.* 乾杯
6 celebratory [ˋsɛləbrə͵torɪ] *adj.* 快樂的；慶祝的

會後分析
Postmortems[1]

☐ You really had us worried there.
你們那時真的讓我們頗為困惱。

☐ You sure do drive a hard bargain.[2]
你們真是很會殺價。

☐ We never thought you'd agree to lower your price.
我們從來沒想到你們會同意降價。

☐ We thought for certain you'd insist on canceling the December order.
我們以為你們一定會堅持要取消十二月的訂單。

☐ We couldn't have lowered our price to twenty-two if it hadn't have been for you making concessions on the minimum order.
如果不是你們在最少訂單量上做了讓步，我們就不可能把價格降到二十二。

☐ Your willingness to separate the issues from the people was the key to us reaching an agreement.
你們願意對事而不對人是我們能夠達成協議的關鍵。

■ postmortem [ˌpostˋmɔrtəm] n. 事後的檢討
■ drive a hard bargain 做一次條件很有利於自己的交易；狠殺（賣主）的價

139

改變心意
A Change of Heart[1]

談不攏？不用怕，因為事情可能不是完全沒有希望，你可能還會有第二次的機會。

☐ Is your offer still on the table?[2]

你們的提議還可以談嗎？

☐ Mr. Jiang has changed his mind.

江先生改變了主意。

☐ My client has had a change of heart.

我的客戶改變了心意。

☐ We'd like to take you up on[3] your offer.

我們想要接受你們的提議。

☐ There's been an unexpected change in plan/personnel/policy.

計畫／人事安排／政策上有出乎意料的變化。

☐ We've reevaluated[4] your proposal/plan and we see its merits.

我們重新評估了你們的提議／計畫，看出了其中的優點。

---

1 change of heart 改變心意
2 on the table 提交考慮
3 take sb. up on 接受某人的（提議等）
4 reevaluate [ˌriˈvæljuˌet] v. 重新評估

國家圖書館出版品預行編目資料

談判 900 句典 / Jason Grenier 作；何岱耘譯.
——初版.——臺北市；貝塔，2006〔民 95〕
　　面：　　公分

　ISBN 978-957-729-614-6（平裝附光碟片）
　1. 商業英語—句法　2. 商業談判

805.169　　　　　　　　　　　　　95022017

談判 900 句典

Overheard During the Negotiation

作　　者 / Jason Grenier
總 編 審 / 王復國
譯　　者 / 何岱耘
執行編輯 / 陳家仁

出　　版 / 貝塔出版有限公司
地　　址 / 台北市 100 館前路 12 號 11 樓
電　　話 / (02)2314-2525
傳　　真 / (02)2312-3535
郵　　撥 / 19493777 貝塔出版有限公司
客服專線 / (02)2314-3535
客服信箱 / btservice@betamedia.com.tw

總 經 銷 / 時報文化出版企業股份有限公司
地　　址 / 桃園縣龜山鄉萬壽路二段 351 號
電　　話 / (02) 2306-6842

出版日期 / 2006 年 12 月初版一刷
定　　價 / 250 元
ISBN-13：978-957-729-614-6
ISBN-10：957-729-614-9

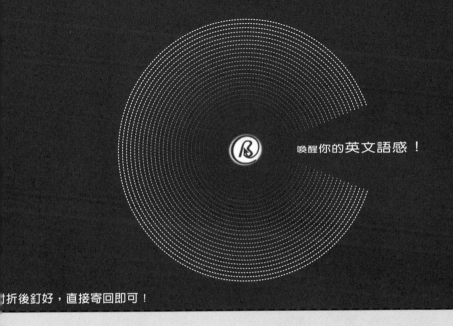

喚醒你的英文語感！

折後釘好，直接寄回即可！

100 台北市中正區館前路12號11樓

貝塔語言出版　收
Beta Multimedia Publishing

寄件者住址 □□□

讀者服務專線（02）2314-3535　讀者服務傳真（02）2312-3535
客戶服務信箱 btservice@betamedia.com.tw

www.betamedia.com.tw

謝謝您購買本書！！
貝塔語言擁有最優良之英文學習書籍，為提供您最佳的英語學習資訊，您填妥此表後寄回（免貼郵票）將可不定期免費收到本公司最新發行書訊及活動訊息！

姓名：＿＿＿＿＿＿＿＿＿　性別：□男□女　生日：＿＿＿＿年＿＿＿＿月＿＿＿＿日

電話：(公)＿＿＿＿＿＿＿＿　(宅)＿＿＿＿＿＿＿＿＿　(手機)＿＿＿＿＿＿＿＿

電子信箱：＿＿＿＿＿＿＿＿＿＿＿＿＿＿＿＿＿＿＿＿＿

學歷：□高中職含以下 □專科 □大學 □研究所含以上

職業：□金融 □服務 □傳播 □製造 □資訊 □軍公教 □出版 □自由 □教育 □學生 □其他

職級：□企業負責人 □高階主管 □中階主管 □職員 □專業人士

1. 您購買的書籍是？＿＿＿＿＿＿＿＿＿＿＿＿＿＿＿＿

2. 您從何處得知本產品？(可複選)

　　□書店 □網路 □書展 □校園活動 □廣告信函 □他人推薦 □新聞報導 □其他

3. 您覺得本產品價格：

　　□偏高 □合理 □偏低

4. 請問目前您每週花了多少時間學英語？

　　□不到十分鐘 □十分鐘以上，但不到半小時 □半小時以上，但不到一小時

　　□一小時以上，但不到兩小時 □兩個小時以上 □不一定

5. 通常在選擇語言學習書時，哪些因素是您會考慮的？

　　□封面 □內容、實用性 □品牌 □媒體、朋友推薦 □價格 □其他＿＿＿＿＿＿＿＿

6. 市面上您最需要的語言書種類為？

　　□聽力 □閱讀 □文法 □口說 □寫作 □其他＿＿＿＿＿＿＿＿

7. 通常您會透過何種方式選購語言學習書籍？

　　□書店門市 □網路書店 □郵購 □直接找出版社 □學校或公司團購

　　□其他＿＿＿＿＿＿＿＿

8. 給我們的建議：＿＿＿＿＿＿＿＿＿＿＿＿＿＿＿＿＿＿＿＿＿

＿＿＿＿＿＿＿＿＿＿＿＿＿＿＿＿＿＿＿＿＿＿＿＿＿＿＿

喚醒你的英文語感！

Get a Feel for English !

喚醒你的英文語感！

Get a Feel for English !